Defiled Innocence

Guy C. Dashnea

authorHOUSE

AuthorHouse™
1663 Liberty Drive
Bloomington, IN 47403
www.authorhouse.com
Phone: 833-262-8899

This is a work of fiction. All of the characters, names, incidents, organizations, and dialogue
in this novel are either the products of the author's imagination or are used fictitiously.

Published by AuthorHouse   08/29/2020

ISBN: 978-1-7283-7253-2 (sc)
ISBN: 978-1-7283-7251-8 (hc)
ISBN: 978-1-7283-7252-5 (e)

Library of Congress Control Number: 2020916786

Print information available on the last page.

Any people depicted in stock imagery provided by Getty Images are models,
and such images are being used for illustrative purposes only.
Certain stock imagery © Getty Images.

This book is printed on acid-free paper.

Foreword

A teenage Metis trapper, reared in the Canadian wilderness, is thrust into civilization in early twentieth century Saskatchewan. Lynes and his family and friends become involved in historical events and interact with actual Prince Albert residents and prominent figures in Canadian history. This saga was inspired by the son of this trapper who wishes he had asked his father more questions about that colorful past while Lynes was still alive.

Guy Courtland Dashnea, author
February 27, 2012

The sweet fragrance of fresh cut hay surrounded the teenager as he approached the barn to begin his first chore of the day. He was filled with excitement in anticipation of the adventure upon which he would embark this warm summer morning. Lynes was well into his teenage years, and his long, gangling, youthful body belied the remarkable strength he possessed. There was solemnity and hardness etched in his face. The innocence of youth kept him from being aware of how extraordinarily handsome he had become. The, deep, dark eyes and straight black hair he had inherited from his Cree Indian (First Nations) mother and French father, Pierre. The latter, a short, stocky Frenchman, had traveled to Northern Saskatchewan in 1889 to trap and homestead.

Pierre met Lynes's mother shortly after he arrived, and the two were soon married. Little Deer That Runs (Apisis lyapiw ana pimpalta) adopted the name, Margarette at Pierre's bidding. As nature would have it, Pierre and Margarette began adding to the population of Saskatchewan. By the time their third child arrived, the parents had a well-established backwoods farm. A 200 square foot log cabin, covered by an abundant sod roof, sat on the edge of a dense emerald forest. Because of its southern exposure, the cabin caught the morning's first light and throughout the day, the welcoming warmth of the sun. A small barn with an attached smokehouse lay a handy fifty feet to the right of the roughly hewn cabin.

All summer long, a thin, light gray vapor rose from the smokehouse only to be captured momentarily like a soft white cloud in the tops of the evergreens. Berry bushes and light shrubbery contrasted with the silver-white bark of birch trees that lined a small river 150 feet to the left of the simple home. A long, wide meadow stretched out in front of the family cabin. In the summer, the field was carpeted with blue-green blades of wild rye. Colorful patterns of wildflowers vied with each other, casting their generous wares in waves of lemon yellow, poppy red, and baby blue in the tall grasses that dotted the landscape. Pierre cultivated an acre of the fertile black soil near the river bank, growing potatoes, corn, dill, cabbage and whatever seeds he could acquire at the trading post. The nearest neighbors were Andrea Beauchene, a trapper 10 miles north, and Little Deer That Runs' family camp seven miles to the southwest.

Lynes's brother Oliver was thirteen months older than he and a year and a half separated Lynes and his younger sister, Madeleine. Oliver was built more like his father, the Metis Cree features more evident in his face and body. Unlike Lynes, a strict and demanding father and the rigors and hardships of the northern frontier had not robbed Oliver of the gaiety and exuberance of youth. From the age of two and until he was nine years old, Oliver was reared in the village of Margarette's father and mother on the Little Red River. A curious, intellectual boy, Oliver pursued his insatiable quest for knowledge. By the age of six, he could read and write the Cree language and was well versed in their religion and legends. He also added the ability to read and write in French and English in a missionary school the Jesuit priests had established near the village although Oliver did so without his Grandfather Big Hand's blessing. Lynes and Oliver's grandfather disliked the Jesuit priest and the Canadian government for, among other things, making it a crime to dance the Sun Dance. Every year and upon special occasions, the brave and his village peoples would convene with relatives and friends from other outlying villages to pray to the "Spirits" for special favors. If there were hard feelings among any of the tribal members, all would be forgiven and the disgruntled would become friends again. Those were the happiest days of Big Hand's youth. When those days were taken from him, the warrior left his village to fight in the "Northwest Rebellion of 1885". When the respected native heard that the Metis and other First Nation Peoples had rebelled against the Canadian government at Duck Lake, he and his best friend, Wild Goose, left Little Red River Village to join in the rebellion.

It was not a simple matter for Big Hand and Wild Goose to leave the comfort of their village; however, they took what pelts they could carry to trade for rifles and ammunition at the trading post near their village. It took every pelt they had in trade just to purchase two Henry rifles and 150 rounds of ammunition. Invigorated, Big Hand left the trading post justly excited that he possessed a weapon of such firepower.

The winter snow blanketed the frozen ground while thick ice still held the rivers captive. Undaunted by the extreme cold, the two young braves struggled through the impervious snow on their noble crusade to free the First Nation Peoples from the oppressive Canadian government. In each village the two friends passed, they encountered other arduous young men who wanted to join their ranks. Learning that other men like him were willing to fight for their freedom, Big Hand determinedly sought the venerated Chief Big Bear. Now a grown man, Big Hand recalled his first meeting as a small child with Big Bear at the Sun Dance in his own village. Stories were told of Big Bear's wisdom and bravery, and how, when the Canadian government sent agents with gifts to get the warrior to sign treaties, the Chief had declined, saying, "When we set a fox trap, we scatter pieces of meat all around, but when the fox gets into the trap, we knock him on the head. We want no bait; let your chiefs come like men and talk to us." It was related that even Sitting Bull had sought Big Bear's wisdom. Eyes and ears alert, Big Hand had never forgotten those stories.

On their journey, Big Hand and Wild Goose met Chief Big Bear for the second time. The Chief, along with his war chief, Wandering Spirit was leading a large war party just one day's walk from the European settlement at Frog Lake. The seasons and the abusive policies of the government had left their mark upon the great leader. Nearing starvation, Big Bear was leading his tribe to confront the Indian Agent at Frog Lake. The objective of the war party was to overpower the settlers and seize supplies vital for sustaining themselves. This occasion marked the first time Big Hand had ever raised his hand against another human being. He rehearsed the mission he was given by Wandering Spirit repeatedly in his mind, unaware that he would be taking part in what would later be known as "The Frog Lake Massacre".

Thomas Quinn, the Indian agent appointed by the government, gave no thought to the welfare of the Indian people. Not only did he treat the Indian people harshly, but he also traded or sold part of the food that was legally supposed to go to them for his personal benefit. Furthermore, he was a cantankerous and stubborn fellow who gave no thought to anyone but himself, a thought obviously misplaced. His good fortune, however, was short lived.

It was early morning when that rascal Quinn heard the loud knock on his cabin door. He thought it might be one of the settlers from the church inquiring if he were going to mass. When he threw open the door, he was surprised to see four Indians with a travois loaded with buffalo robes. Wandering Spirit, Little Bad Man, (Ayemasis, Big Bear's son), Iron Body, and Big Hand humbled themselves before the agent to gain his trust. Knowing that the agent's greed would overcome his caution, Wandering Spirit offered the buffalo robes in trade for a few pounds of pemmican (dry pounded meat, berries, and melted animal fat). When all Indians were inside the cabin with an armload of robes, Wandering Spirit gave the signal and the Indians quickly overpowered the agent.

Outside, 100 warriors concealed in the brush, surrounded the settlement. When Wandering Spirit gave a hand signal, the waiting war part quietly converged on the church. The warriors deftly tied Quinn's hands, gagged him with a mouth full of pemmican, secured with a strap of rawhide and watched unmoved as a rivulet of spit slowly made its way from the agent's forehead, hanging like a pendulum from the imprisoned scoundrel's chin. Little Bad Man had succeeded in making his long restrained resentments known.

Both Big Hand and Iron Body, avengers of past grievances, dragged Quinn, struggling like a fresh caught trout, to the steps of the church. When Big Bear and 20 armed Indians burst through the church door, an ear-piercing scream punctured the air. Mothers threw their bodies over their children, and grown men stood in shock and trepidation uncertain of the next move of their assailants. Father Leon Fafard's voice could be detected over the whoops and hollers of the inflamed Indians, telling the settlers to keep calm and not make any sudden moves that would further incite the warriors. Suddenly, Big Bear stepped up beside the priest and raised his hand. In an instant, an eerie silence fell over the congregation. Big Hand's eyes fell upon the skinned out bear claws resting on Big Bear's chest. They were his talisman that protected him and gave him powerful medicine. Big Bear then spoke to the frightened settlers, admonishing them to go peacefully with his braves. The great warrior knew the government was in pursuit, and he intended on using the settlers as hostages.

Finally, Quinn wrested the pemmican gag from his mouth and started screaming to the settlers, telling them that when they reached the woods, they would all be slaughtered. The terrified agent, essentially incoherent by now and reaching the point of hysteria, abruptly ceased his exhortations and crumpled inertly to the floor--a well-placed rifle ball had blown off the back of his head. Instantly, in one enormous leap forward, Big Bear snatched the rifle from Wandering Spirit's hands, but it was too late. Other braves, thinking it was a signal, began firing into the crowd of settlers. Father Fafard and Father Marchand tried to shield their parishioners but both were shot dead. After the ensuing melee, Big Hand left the church and sat with Big Bear and the remaining hostages. He did not participate in the Scalp Dance, and from that moment on, the brave seldom left Big Bear's side.

After the unfortunate incident at the church, Wandering Spirit sent out scouts to cover their trail. Both he and Big Bear realized by now that it was hopeless to engage the large number of troops that would be searching for them. The men were well aware of the cannons, Gatling guns, and seemingly, endless supplies their enemy possessed. The braves' only hope for survival lay to the north where they could lose themselves in the wilderness. The trail was long and hard, and the hostages survived only because they were protected by Big Bear and Big Hand. When the desperate group were able to rest at last, Big Bear decided that Frenchman's Butte would be a good defensive encampment. The decision was not without controversy; however, because of Big Bear's attempt to stop the killing at Frog Lake, and his concern regarding the safety of the hostages, he had lost favor with Wandering Spirit and the latter's son, Little Bad Man, and some braves who condoned the massacre at Frog Lake.

Little Bad Man's anger kindled when Big Bear commanded, "We will rest here."

With only inches between him and his father, Little Bad Man sneered, "You will no longer make decisions for me or anyone else.

You are too old, and you have become a coward. Stay with the white man you have been protecting and love so much. Your place is with the dogs!" Little Bad Man had a habit of spitting to show his contempt or disapproval and did so now, spitting right into Big Bear's face.

Standing by, Big Hand watched disapprovingly as Little Bad Man shouted at Big Bear, his own father. When Little Bad Man spat disrespectfully into Big Bear's face, Big Hand flew into a blinding rage. There was no thought of time or space, nothing, only an all-consuming rage that drove him to seek vengeance upon Little Bad Man. Big Hand woke from this oblivion to find himself on top of Little Bad Man, knife in hand, only to be restrained by Big Bear himself. In spite of Big Hand's efforts to defend his chief, many of the young braves scorned Big Bear and turned to their war chief, Wandering Spirit to lead them. Those who had fought with Big Bear fifteen years earlier against the Blackfeet at Belly River remained his loyal followers.

At Wandering Spirit's insistence, the tribal members and hostages moved on into the night. Three miles from Frenchman's Butte, the 500 fleeing Cree along with their captives encountered a field of muskeg. By the time half the people crossed, the permafrost gave way, leaving the rest of the band stranded in a sea of black, rotting fauna. It took a Herculean effort and many hours of labor to set the stranded free. The tribes were exhausted from the ordeal and had to stop and rest. Big Hand threw out the soft beaver blanket his mother had made for him earlier. He reflected fondly upon the Sun Dance. He discovered that sleep came easier if he turned his thoughts to those happy past days. The snoring of Big Bear lying next to him was not an annoying sound; it was comforting to know that the old warrior was sleeping peacefully. Big Hand had just drifted off into a welcomed slumber when the shouts of Wandering Spirit and his braves awakened him. The arriving braves had just learned that their pursuers were no more than two hours behind them. Obviously, their camp was not in a tenable position to fight as the people were too exhausted to travel any farther. Wandering Spirit would take 200 warriors back to Frenchman's Butte where he would attempt to hold off the government troops while Big Bear would stay to defend what was left of their scattered tribe.

Big Bear urged, "Go with Wandering Spirit and watch out for my son, Little Bad Man. I don't want him to die, hating his father."

It was at Frenchman's Butte that Big Hand became known as a fearless and skillful warrior. Upon arrival at the location, Big Hand chose a position near Little Bad Man, a shallow gully where the enemy would not easily see him. A soft shuffling sound could be heard as Wandering Spirit positioned his warriors and then a stark silence hung in the dark morning air. Less than a half hour passed when the creaking of wagon wheels penetrated the distance. As the sound grew closer, Big Hand strained his eyes trying to see any movement in the dark shadows. So intense was he that he was startled when a hand gripped his shoulder. It was Wandering Spirit.

"I have seen that you are a good friend of Big Bear. He was once a great chief. I hope he has sent his big medicine with you," with that statement the war chief quickly melted into the darkness.

As the morning progressed, Big Hand could see the government troops not more than a thousand yards from his position. Without warning, the enemy disappeared in an instant behind a cloud of smoke. Just as suddenly, the ground shook and rocks flew through the air. The sound of a thousand tree branches snapping, mingled with the echoes of thunderous cannon balls exploding, one at the very crest of the gully in which Big hand crouched. The impact of the exploding ball knocked him to the ground, causing a harsh ringing in his ears. Swiftly, Big hand jumped to his feet and began firing back.

After three hours of pitched battle, Wandering Spirit and his warriors were almost out of ammunition. In an attempt to capture the enemy supply wagons, Big Hand led a party of warriors to flank the government troops. Their attack was so fierce and bold, the government forces retreated, thinking they were outnumbered and expecting to be attacked from the rear. As the Indians hurried back to join up with their tribes, Wandering Spirit came to Big Hand and said, "It is good that Big Bear sent his medicine with you." Not one Cree had been wounded or even killed during the battle.

Big Bear smiled when he saw Big Hand. "I see you did good work watching out for Little Bad Man."

"It was your medicine that did it."

Big Bear just turned his head and smiled. Six days later as the tribe reached Loon Lake, they faced the Northwest Mounted Police and the Alberta Mounted Rifles. The Cree had used up almost all of their bullets and powder during the battle at Frenchman's Butte. In an emergency council meeting, Big Hand and Wandering Spirit, realizing that the situation had become hopeless, instructed the warriors on how to avoid capture if they were encountered, "Those who have no ammunition and can no longer fight, spread out in all directions and save yourselves."

When the joint government forces opened fire upon the tribe, Big Hand and Wild Goose answered back, using the last bullets they had left for their Henry's. Most of the warriors were carrying muskets, and they continued the fight on until they ran out of powder. Whenever Big Hand and his friend, Wild Goose, ran out of ammunition, they fled to their horses. Big Bear, however, refused to leave with them. Instead, he stood up and began to walk leisurely between the two adversaries. Exploding rifle balls, whizzing bullets, and acrid smoke filled the air. Like a ghost, Big Bear would disappear in a cloud of smoke and reappear momentarily, only to disappear again. The heated battle was still raging as Big Bear vanished at last into the tree line.

Another Metis trapper, Edward DeGrace, followed Big Hand and Wild Goose when those two escaped from the Battle at Loon Lake. Sometime previously, Ed had become a hostage of Big Bear at the Battle of Fort Pitt. Fortunately, Big Bear saved his life when the trapper was about to be killed by two hotheaded warriors. In another fracas, Ed's life was spared at Frog Lake when Big Hand thwarted another attempt upon his life at the Scalp Dance. Ed, a man of principle and compassion, had also fought with Dumont at the Battle of Duck Lake just six days previously. The fighters had defeated the government troops, and then Ed traveled to Fort Pitt to spy on the Northwest Mounted Police. The trapper had always been sympathetic toward the Indians' plight and considered them his allies. Out of respect and admiration, he followed Big Hand and his friend.

When Big Hand and Wild Goose reached their village, they were greeted with spontaneous cheers and rough backslapping. Once again, Big Hand, happy to be home, settled into the peaceful every day functions of the village, but the horrors of war, and his hatred for the Canadian government remained with him.

In the meantime, Big Hand refused to allow Oliver to go to the Jesuit missionary school, but Oliver's thirst for knowledge would not be denied. Finally, after weeks of pleading with his father, Oliver slipped away from his village and enrolled in the mission. Big Hand, remembering what Big Bear had said to him about his own son at the Battle of Frenchman's Butte, ("Watch out for my son, I don't want him to die, hating his father."), held his tongue and said a prayer to his God, Kice-Manito, for Oliver.

While Oliver attended the mission school every chance he had, his younger brother Lynes attended his daily chores, the large bay draft horse now whinnying a welcome at the first sight of Lynes. Cheval's massive body gentled pushed the smaller saddle horse away from the manger; he knew that when Lynes emerged from the barn, breakfast would be served. Giving Cheval one half gallon of oats in the early morning was Lynes's first chore of the day. Rouge, the sorrel mustang, only received a handful of oats because there was no work for him today. Both Lynes and Oliver were required to feed all the farm critters before they could enjoy their own morning meal. While the gentle giant munched his oats, Lynes brushed the dirt and debris from the massive body. It was a daily task as Cheval delighted in rolling around in the shade of the barn to gain relief from the sweltering heat. Lynes dutifully harnessed Cheval, hooking him up to the wagon, as he continued thinking upon the exciting adventure coming up after breakfast.

The only sound at the breakfast table was that of the knife and fork and an occasional smacking of the lips. No one dared speak during a Dashneaux meal, and no one dared leave the table until everyone had finished. Having eaten everything on his plate (another Dashneaux edict), Lynes mused in silence, impatiently waiting for his father to push his chair away from the table. When Pierre glanced across the table into his young son's eyes, a knowing smile flashed across his face. It was a tender, loving smile that Lynes caught only upon rare occasions.

The only time Lynes had taken the 35 mile journey to Prince Albert was three years ago, but every footstep was engraved in his mind. He had the innate ability to remember every rock, tree, broken branch, or trodden soil between the family farm and Prince Albert. Since he was no more than eight years old, he had gleefully accompanied his father, laying out trap lines that extended as far as 20 miles afield. That previous winter, Lynes had proven his strength and courage. When he and his father were approaching a "deadfall trap" on their trap line, a wolverine broke loose and attacked Pierre. Without hesitation, Lynes jumped upon the wolverine's back and killed it with his knife. Fortunately, the heavy buffalo robe and wool pants under a pair of buckskin outer pants kept Pierre from serious injury. Pierre had wisely chosen his son for this trip because he had come to rely on Lynes's keen perception and his known capability in handling any unseen problems.

Pierre did not check the wagon out to see if it was ready for the trip nor did he look to see if the needed tools and equipment were aboard. He was fully confident that Lynes had everything well in hand. Fur pelts and blankets were stacked and well secured for the arduous journey ahead. Ordinarily, Pierre would transport the winter catch in his canvas cargo canoe. A tributary of the Shellbrook River ran through his homestead and wound its way to the Sturgeon River and then on to the North Saskatchewan River. This year the trapper would have furs from the village as well as his own. Better prices were always given for furs in Prince Albert.

Not a word was spoken as Pierre climbed aboard the loaded wagon and sat down beside his young son. Warmth and security welled inside Lynes when, for the second time, father and son's eyes met, and a gentle smile swept his father's face. Pierre looked back at Oliver, "Keep the shotgun loaded."

When the wagon left the Dashneaux homestead, it entered a dense conifer forest, criss-crossed by streams and shallow rivers that would find their way to what the First Nations called, Kisiskaciwani-Sipiy, (Fast Flowing River), a perfect description for the 800-mile long North Saskatchewan River. The sun had just begun its trek across a cloudless sky, its golden beams shone through the branches, capturing the cool moist air to form mystical patterns across the winding trail. The haunting hoot of the loon and the sporadic rat-tat-tat of the woodpecker blended with the constant rattle of the harness and wagon as it labored its way through the woods. Three years had passed since the wagon had negotiated the narrow trail. There were frequent interruptions-- windfall removals and brush cutting to allow the vehicle to pass.

Afternoon shadows crossed the trail, and the slight drop in temperature brought out the insects to torment man and beast. Lynes knew that before it became too dark to continue on, he and his father would reach a Cree hunting party encampment that he remembered was not too far ahead. A ponderous load of furs and the rough terrain were a challenge, even for a splendid horse such as Cheval. Even now, the sleek brown hair on the horse's broad chest and neck glistened with sweat. The Percheron-Shire mix gave Lynes's four-footed prized animal the heart, stamina, and strength to overcome such adversity. It would be another long, difficult day on the unbeaten path before it intersected with the well-trodden common trail used by trappers, loggers, and Indians.

When Lynes and Pierre reached the campsite, they could tell that it had been occupied not more than an hour before their arrival. Mattresses of fresh cut boughs lay under the shelters that were scattered around the clearing. Chavel stood motionless, as his ears perked up and his nostrils flared. A gentle tug on Pierre's arm and a familiar knowing look in his son's eyes prompted the father to reach for his trusty Henry rifle. For several seconds the two sat in silence. Lynes felt a quiet apprehension as he triggered all his senses to absorb each sound and movement in the forest surrounding the camp. Not a phrase was spoken as Lynes and Pierre slowly stepped down from the wagon. Quietly yet deftly, Lynes released the tugs from the singletree and led Cheval around to tie him to the back of the wagon. In unison, father and son crawled under the wagon and waited in silence. Slowly, the rustling crush of dry leaves and the occasional snap of a broken twig began to spread out in front of the two men. Experience told them it was not the sound of foraging animals.

Pierre had good reason for feeling anxious as he lay prone under the wagon. Two seasons ago, he had the misfortune of running into pirates on the Shellbrook River. Pierre had loaded his cargo canoe with almost a ton of valuable furs as he effortlessly negotiated the gently flowing river, all the while lazily admiring the tall stands of aspen, birch, and jack pine that lined the banks. The new foliage on the aspen fluttered silver and green in the warm summer breeze, emitting a soothing whispering sigh. A majestic bald eagle invaded the picturesque scene as it swooped down to perch on top of a towering jack pine. As Pierre drew his attention from the eagle, he caught a fleeting glimpse of an intruder standing back in the woods. When he did a double take, no one was there.

The canoe drifted another 100 feet downstream. Then Pierre observed movement through the thick branches along the stream. Another 200 feet passed and the alert trapper again sighted a man stealthily moving through the timber. Adrenaline shot through Pierre's body at the realization that he had become prey. He knew that in the bend of the river just ahead lay another danger. A rocky sandbar choked off the river's natural flow, narrowing the stream to no more than 20 feet width. The wild rush of water through the chute opened up again in 50 feet then settled back into the gentle character of the Shellbrook. The furs would have to be portaged across the sandbar to avoid the dangers of the chute. It was no surprise to Pierre when the expected sandbar emerged into view, only this time a fallen tree crossed the narrow passageway. Pierre quickly assessed his choices.

There was no place above the chute to beach the canoe. The rocky sandbar was his only choice. Just before the craft scraped bottom, Pierre, rifle in hand, leaped into the river, keeping the pelt-laden canoe between him and the woods. At the same instant he leaped out of the canoe, a loud report came from behind a tree less than 100 feet away. By the sound and the amount of smoke that filled the air, Pierre recognized a musket. He stepped from behind the furs to return fire before his assailant had time to reload. Another musket fired from behind a jack pine four feet from where the first shot came. Pierre rested the Henry across the bow of the canoe, waiting for the smoke to clear. The black powder had not quite dissipated when Pierre sighted buckskin-clad legs below the haze. He knew he hit his mark when he heard the dull thud and an audible moan. The icy water began to bite his legs. Checking the breach of his Henry, the trapper waded to the other end of the canoe. With the barrel of the rifle, Pierre slowly raised a layer of beaver pelts until he could see through the slit.

The slight movement of a pine branch gave Pierre the location of the second pirate, but the culprit was not exposed enough for Lynes's father to get off a clear shot. Just a few feet away from the second pirate, Pierre caught a glimpse of buckskin-clad legs rolling around in the brush and the subsequent sounds of gasping, moaning, and pleadings for help. Pierre knew he had to act fast before his own legs became numb and useless. Taking a chance that there were only two pirates, he stepped out from behind his canoe and jumped back just in time to hear the musket ball crack through the air. Judging that he could reach his assailant before the thief could reload his musket, Pierre charged at the man as fast as he could run in mukluks filled with water. The pirate had just put the powder down the muzzle of his musket when he realized the trapper was half way across the sandbar, racing toward him. As the robber turned to flee, Pierre stopped, took aim, and pulled the trigger just as the marauder disappeared into the woods.

When Pierre entered the woods, he found a Springfield musket, lock plate and hammer destroyed and black powder still inside the bore. To his right lay an unfortunate, suffering Indian. The round from the Henry had hit him just above the groin. His face was twisted in pain, and his hands were red with blood as he was holding himself as if to stop a bowel movement. The youngster's face was so contorted in pain it took Pierre a second to recognize him. The boy was from his wife, Margarette's village.

At that moment, a myriad of conflicting emotions like those that he had never known before, swept over Pierre. On the other hand, the guilt, anger, compassion, and frustration instantly disappeared when the trapper spied his valuable cargo slowly drifting away from the sandbar. If the canoe were drawn into the chute, it would be caught on the tree and dragged under by the current. Frantically, Pierre raced across the sandbar and strode into the frigid river. Water rose well above his waist as he reached the canoe. Swiftly, Pierre secured the cargo on the sandbar as the groans and screams from shore filled the air. Reluctantly, Pierre walked toward the suffering young man. As Pierre reached down and picked up a club-like piece of driftwood, he began questioning the morality of what he felt he had to do.

13

While the gentle current carried the winter's catch down the Shellbrook River, Pierre wondered if he would have covered the young body with river rock had the youth not been from Margarette's village. A sudden chill ran over Lynes's body at the crack of a rifle and whoops and hollers emanating out of the darkness of the outlying woods. Pierre recognized one of the voices; he looked at Lynes.

"Big Hand! Trou-du-cul! (You asshole!).

Pierre's voice boomed, "Big Hand, trou-du-cul! (Big Hand, You asshole!)."

A roar of laughter burst out of the forest as did Big Hand, four of his braves, and Ed DeGrace. When Big Hand emerged from the woods, his laughter exposed every line, wrinkle, and crevice in his weathered face. In the darkness of the evening shadows, the object Big Hand was holding was indistinguishable. As he drew closer, Lynes and Pierre were able to discern that Big Hand had his pipe stone bundle, "Askitci"(stem of a pipe not to be used for smoking) in his outstretched hand. Father and son were aware that they dare not show anger if "Askitci" were presented to them. It would not be wise to insult a prestigious warrior like Big Hand.

Lynes was delighted to see his grandfather, and Pierre was relieved that the group were not more pirates. Accepting the prank, the hunting party was greeted with handshakes and much laughter. Chewing on pemmican and eating berries along the trail was the only food Lynes and Pierre had eaten that day. Hence, the two welcomed Big Hand's invitation to share in the fruits of their hunt. As the flames licked the flesh of a fresh killed moose, they cast an eerie shimmering light upon everything that surrounded the camp. The faces and clothing of the men gathered around the fire were a reflection of the north woods of Saskatchewan. Big Hand and his braves totally garbed in buckskin, beaver and fox, contrasted sharply with the white man's clothing worn by Pierre and Lynes.

As was customary after the small talk was finished and the meal over, each would have his turn, telling a story or legend around the fire. Pierre kept a pouch of tobacco that was only opened upon such special occasions. When he pulled out the pouch and gingerly filled his pipe, big smiles crossed the faces of Big Hand and his party. As the glowing bowl was passed, the ritual began. Lynes anticipated that his grandfather would tell a tale about Big Bear and the war in 1885. In turn, Pierre would relate the story about his encounter with the pirates on the Shellbrook River, omitting the identity of the young man he had been forced to slay. Ed DeGrace, upon hearing the story, offered to accompany Lynes and Pierre on their trip to Prince Albert. It would be unlikely that anyone would be foolhardy enough to stand up to two Henry rifles. Without the protection of the river, the land route to Prince Albert gave rogues and thieves more opportunities to engage in their mischief. Pierre was eager to accept Ed's generous offer. In peace, the two of them sat well into the night, telling stories and sipping whiskey that Pierre had brewed from the berries that grew along the river.

As the dawning light began to filter through the jack pines, the campers began to stir. Lynes was giving Cheval his breakfast of oats while he listened to the wilderness awaken from the sounds of the night. The ravens' call and the chickadees' chirping blended in with the chattering of a pair of squirrels frolicking in the upper branches of the jack pine. A spider's web on a nearby shelter caught the early morning dew and sparkled like threaded diamonds, shimmering in the cool morning breeze. Cooked moose meat, remnants of the fire, and stories from the previous night, still hung in the air. Lynes held on to the inner joy he felt from spending the evening with friends and relatives he loved.

As the group journeyed on, Ed DeGrace, who was a robust man full of energy and commitment, attacked the brush and windfalls that hindered their progress as if his life depended upon it. Because of Ed's inexhaustible efforts, the travelers would reach the well-trod route to Prince Albert sooner than Lynes expected. As they continued down the trail, nothing was as Lynes imagined. At times, the men filled the deep ruts in the sandy soil with branches so the wagon could pass. Such interruptions gave Lynes time to think about the small village where his mother had relatives and where he had been challenged by an Indian boy, the two of them chasing each other around the site. Soon, this wagon party would be stopping there. Lynes remembered that a dozen wigwams sat in a large grass-covered field with gardens, smoke racks, and hide frames populating the terrain. The landscape before him reminded him of a story that only now, did Lynes understand, and it became clear to him why his uncle stared at him when he narrated the tale of "The Warriors of The Rainbow." The words flooded his mind as his thoughts drifted.

"One hundred years ago, a wise old woman named Eyes of Fire had a vision of the future. She prophesied that one day, because of the white man's (Yo-ne-gis) greed, there would come a time when the earth, ravaged and polluted, the forests having been destroyed, the birds would fall from the air; the waters would blacken; the fish would lie poisoned in the streams; the trees would no longer exist, and mankind as then known, would cease to be. In such a time, the keepers of the legends, tales, cultural rituals, and all the ancient tribal customs would be needed to restore humankind and the earth to good health, and make the earth green again. The natives would be humanity's key to survival; they were the Warriors of The Rainbow. The day of awakening would come when all the peoples of all the tribes would form a "New World of Justice," peace, freedom, and recognition of the Great Spirit. The "Warriors of The Rainbow" would spread these messages and teach all peoples of the earth ("Elohi") how to live the way of the Great Spirit. They would remind them of how the world had turned away from the Great Spirit and that is why the earth is sick. These Warriors would assure the peoples of the earth that the Great Spirit is full of love and understanding and in doing so would teach them how to make the earth beautiful again. The Warriors would instruct the peoples on morals so that they could live the way the Great Spirit desired them to live. The earth people would then learn to live together in harmony and demonstrate love and understanding among themselves. Like the ancient tribes, the Warriors would teach the peoples how to pray like the Great Spirit with the bounteous love that flows like the beautiful mountain stream that wends along its path to the ocean. Once again, the people would be able to feel joy in solitude, freedom from petty jealousies, and happiness in their hearts. All humankind would love each other regardless of race or religion. Filling their minds and hearts with the purest of thoughts, their hands with the most noble of deeds, the peoples would seek strength and beauty in prayer and solitude. Their children would once again be able to run free, enjoy the natural treasures of Mother Earth, and conquer the toxins and destruction wrought by the white man and his greed. Rivers would run clear, the forests expand, and the plants and animals flourish. Once more, the vital role of all creatures and the plants that sustain them would be respected and preserved so that all that is beautiful would become a way of life. As a daily practice, brothers and sisters of the earth would take care of the needs of the poor, sick, and needy. The leaders of the people would be chosen in the old way, not by their political party, not by the loudest, not by the most boastful, not by name-calling, but by those whose actions spoke the loudest and set the good examples. Those individuals who demonstrated their love, wisdom, and courage and who showed that they could and did work for the common good would be chosen as the chiefs. They would be selected by their virtues, not the amount of money they had obtained. Such leaders would see that the young were educated with the love and wisdom of their surroundings, that they could heal their world of its ills and restore it to its former good health and beauty. The tasks of these Warriors are many and great; mountains of ignorance must be conquered against the walls of prejudice and hatred. In spite of the obstacles, these Warriors must dedicate themselves to the tasks ahead with unwavering conviction and strong hearts. They will find willing hearts and open-minded followers on this road of returning Mother Earth to beauty and bountifulness once more. THE DAY WILL COME; IT IS NOT FAR AWAY."

Having recalled his uncle's tale as his mind drifted, Lynes accepted with clarity now just how much people owed their very existence to the native tribes who had kept their culture and heritage alive through the re-telling of the legends. It would be with such inherited knowledge that humanity would find the key to survival.

Laying aside his meandering thoughts, Lynes observed the wide expanses on both sides of the trail, which were dotted with decaying tree stumps. Dead branches and toppled treetops lay in total disarray, scattered carelessly about where life once sprung from a lush forest floor. All brown now and dry. The young jack pine that had no value was left uprooted, broken, and injured. In spite of the devastation, an occasional jack pine stood upright as if in outright defiance of the woodsman's ax. Large open spaces along the river were cleared of all living matter;

stockpiles of logs waiting to be floated down to the sawmill in Prince Albert, now the only intruders. Lynes contemplated how long it would be before the logging company would invade his own hunting grounds as well as his grandfather's village.

The men met few travelers as they continued their way south; most people traveled north on riverboats that supplied the missions, Hudson Bay Company, and others that engaged in the fur industry. It would be another day on the trail before the group would arrive in Prince Albert. In anticipation, Lynes was eager to see all the buildings, the people garbed in fancy clothing, the gadgets, and unusual machines that performed tasks that were accomplished by hand in his world. As the boy lay wrapped in his soft beaver skin blanket that night, pleasant thoughts of his mother lulled him to sleep.

In another part of the countryside, a young Indian girl, Little Deer That Runs, dreamed of a brave that had the courage, understanding, steadfastness, and faith that she saw in her father. She had been a pretty, chubby, and equally stubborn and adventurous child growing up. At ten years, she insisted on joining her father on hunting parties and even running his trap lines. She was already proficient in every traditional task expected of a grown Cree woman, and it took days of counseling to convince her that the village needed her. Of all the tasks expected of her, Little Deer That Runs favored trapping small game, birds, and catching fish with her mother. At 16, she had grown into a statuesque, lovely young woman. High cheek bones complemented her Cleopatra shaped face; large black eyes, a haughty nose, and thick, silky black hair that flowed below her waist, framed her full soft lips. Although the maid was very popular among the young braves in her village, none of them had the courage to ask for her hand. The braves were apprehensive of approaching Big Hand and the girl's mother "Waskincipekinam" (Walks On Water) foremost, but equally daunting, Little Deer That Runs' fierce independence and indifference to the braves posed the greatest challenge. She was the only child of Big Hand who gave into her every whim. At Little Deer That Runs' insistence, there was little that the father had not taught her. Breaking with tradition and without criticism from the tribe, Big Hand often took the girl with him on hunting parties. It was on such a hunting party that Little Deer met Pierre.

Big Hand became aware of Pierre the summer before while he and Ed DeGrace were themselves on a hunting party. They were also scouting out a trap line for the winter season. Their curiosity was peaked when they observed smoke rising in the distance. Upon arriving at the edge of the wide-open meadow, Big Hand was visibly disturbed that a white man was encroaching on, what he believed, was his land. Pierre scanned the two horsemen sitting motionless at the edge of the meadow, one pulling a travois. Pierre disappeared briefly into a canvas covered, oversized wigwam then reappeared, holding his smoking pipe in his outstretched hand. When the equestrians entered the meadow, the tall grass obscured the horses' legs. As they trotted slowly forward, the entourage appeared to be floating upon waves in a blue-green sea. Pierre was impressed by the magnificent horses the men rode as well as the buckskins of one of the riders.

The buckskin shirt in question was trimmed in finely woven porcupine quills. Below each shoulder, four vertical strips of white rabbit fur were sewed. Just below the strips of rabbit, a continuous stripe of rabbit claws ran from armpit to armpit. On both sides of the chest, bright flower motifs with green vines and leaves adorned the shirtfront. Between the flowers and leaves, two white triangles rose to meet in the center. The sleeves and bottom of the shirt were fringed in black. Big Hand, the object of Pierre's scrutiny, was proud to wear the buckskin shirt that "Little Deer That Runs" had made for him.

Pierre noted that both riders carried Henry rifles across the withers of their mounts, the latter decorated with strips of bear fur, osprey, and eagle feathers. It wasn't until the pair stopped within ten feet of Pierre that he recognized Ed DeGrace. The two of them had met briefly on the Yellowstone River while on their way to the Rendezvous in Idaho in 1883. Pierre was only twenty years old at the time and much of what he learned from Ed DeGrace proved beneficial in later years. However, neither man acknowledged that they had met before.

Big Hand dismounted, rifle in hand, and stepped quickly to within arm's reach of Pierre. At each stride, his long braids swayed across his broad chest, one braid having woven into it, three dazzling blue wing feathers from a Mallard duck and a small, snow-white tail feather from a bald eagle. The Indian hunter was slightly taller than the French settler was and much better dressed. Big Hand stood silent, glaring into Pierre's dark eyes. Then, the warrior was disarmed as his eyes slowly dropped to the pipe Pierre was extending in his outstretched hand. His deep-rooted faith and honor for his traditions would not allow Big Hand to reject Pierre's offer of goodwill.

"Atamisk-atowin." (Greetings.)

Still seething inside, Big Hand turned to Ed DeGrace and motioned for him to dismount and join them. As the trio sat down to smoke the pipe, Big Hand began to make it clear that he did not want Pierre to live in what he believed to be his tribe's hunting grounds. The conversation ended abruptly when Pierre stated that the government sent him to mark out 160 acres, and they would be up shortly to see that he did what was requested of him. (Dominion Land Act--1872). Big Hand's face was expressionless as he rose without saying a word, mounted his horse, and rode off. As he and Ed DeGrace disappeared into the woods, Pierre stood, musing whether or not Big Hand was going to make mischief for him.

Winter arrived early that year. Pierre had watched the birch and aspen growing along his river surrender their gold, orange, and scarlet leaves to the shortened days and the crisp cold call of winter. The barren branches gave the appearance of veins and arteries of Mother Earth against a stark gray sky. It was well past the time to scout out his trap lines for the season, but Pierre had been focused on preparing logs and other materials for the cabin he planned on building in the spring. Upstream from his homestead, the river was fraught with tributaries and channels that provided ideal habitat for beaver, muskrat, fox, and mink. No more than one-quarter mile upstream, five well-established beaver lodges emerged from a large pond the critters had established as their home. All trap sets had to be marked by a Story Pole, a tall, dead branch or stick anchored so the trap set location could be found in the deep snow. When Pierre strode up to the pond, his suspicion that Big Hand was going to make life hard for him was confirmed. Every lodge, channel or possible location for a trap set was distinctly marked by a Story Pole, implying ownership. Big Hand, after a full day's scouting and hiking five miles upriver, claimed Pierre's river as one of his trap lines for that winter.

A long, hard spell of arctic air gripped Pierre's world. He readied himself for the tortuous trek that lay ahead. It would take the better part of a day to check his first trap. He could expect a three-mile hike up river and another two miles up a tributary. There was no need for snowshoes as the trapper headed out to check his trap line. Sub-zero temperatures built a deep-crusted snow he could walk upon, now frozen so thoroughly that there was a squeaking sound at every step. Tiny crystals of frozen air danced like diamonds in the sun, limiting his vision to no more than 50 feet. In the still of the morning, all that Pierre could hear was the sound of his footsteps and the hiss of his toboggan as he pulled it over the ice-packed snow. Every half hour or so, he would stop to rest for a moment and break the frost from his eyebrows and eyelashes, this phenomenon formed by his breath as it froze under his parka's hood.

As the day progressed, the shroud of frozen air gave way intermittently to the scarce sun. Still bitterly chilled, Pierre continued on his journey lest he lose the body heat he produced as he trudged upriver. One-day-old toboggan tracks told Pierre that Big Hand or Ed DeGrace was not too far ahead. Earlier that day when Pierre approached the beaver pond just above his own homestead, he determined that all the traps had been checked to verify if they were triggered. They would be the last beavers harvested on Big Hand's trap line. A seldom seen smile spread across Pierre's face as he contemplated the reaction of Big Hand, if indeed it were he who discovered the pouch of tobacco his adversary had hung from one of the Story Poles.

After Pierre reached the end of his trap line, he was gratified that 90 per cent of his beaver traps had been triggered. Pierre's spirits lifted up when he found that his trap sets for mink and fox had given him a respectable yield. It took Pierre three days to harvest and reset his traps. With a toboggan laden with pelts, Pierre was anxious to return to his homestead. It was late morning when the trapper approached the estuary of the tributary on which his trap line was set. An unkindness of ravens was performing acrobatics in the immobile sky about 300 feet upstream. The raucous birds, silhouetted against an ominous gray sky, soared, dived, and swooped in all directions as if in a frenzy. The quiet of the wilderness ratcheted into pandemonium as the birds' ear splitting squawking and cawing overwhelmed the senses. This was not the first time Pierre had witnessed such a spectacle. He recognized that the din meant danger or tragedy and that whatever its identity, he could not flee. Cautiously, he approached the focus of the aerial display. Pierre noted that hungry timber wolves were restlessly slinking around, keeping some distance from the carcass of a large bull moose. A toboggan loaded with pelts sat a few feet from the dead beast. The wolves' attention was on the carcass; they were not aware that Pierre was watching them. When one of the more aggressive wolves crept menacingly toward the fallen moose, a strident scream that could be heard above the ravens' clamor, rang out. The wolves scattered promptly when Pierre fired off his Henry and approached the corpse.

"Wichihin!" (Help me.), cried the voice that came from the moose.

Pierre was not prepared for the ghastly sight exposed before him. Frost-covered entrails, frozen in the crimson and yellow ice of blood and bile covered the ground. A massive arm extruded from the inside of the wooly beast, skinning knife held rigidly in the extended hand. A Henry rifle and several empty cartridges told Pierre the story of this tableau. And so the story unfolded.

Big Hand had been harvesting his trap line as he pulled his toboggan down the frozen river. A large cow moose startled him when she burst out of the tree line and ran across his path no more than eight feet in front of him. When the moose crossed, she stopped and stood watching Big Hand. From within the aspen forest, two long, sneering, raspy sounds emanated from the cow as if she were taunting the trapper. Suspicious, Big Hand wondered if it might be the spirit "Wisakecahk," (wee-sah-keh-chahk), a trickster in Cree legend that could take the shape of an animal or plant. Big Hand considered what mischief Wisakechahk was up to. His thoughts were shattered by the abrupt sound of broken saplings and shattered brush behind him. He turned just in time to view a massive, dark gray figure just inches away. The trapper felt a dull shock in his left shoulder as an antler knocked him to the ground. As Big Hand rolled to avoid the slashing hooves, he held up the Henry with his right arm to block the oncoming blows. The effort to protect himself did minimal good; his left arm dangled like an autumn leaf hung in the wind. When he rolled, he was caught in the back by the full weight of a striking hoof. Big Hand felt no pain, just numbness that left his lower body useless. Once again the huge beast struck, raising itself on its hind legs to deliver its final blow, which left Big Hand helpless. From that moment on, the world outside existed in a time warp to the trapper. The slashing hooves beat a slow and graceful staccato. The blasting flow of freezing breath from the nostrils of the great bull moose became a whisper floating away, only to be lost in the icy air. In a last ditch effort, Big Hand raised his Henry, the stock half buried in the snow, pointed it at the hulk above him and fired. The heart exploded inside the beast, but the life force refused to leave his body as once again the deadly hooves came down missing Big Hand by inches. The long legs folded under the weight of the beast, dropping 1300 pounds of flesh and blood upon the unfortunate Indian. All the air was crushed from his lungs as the bull moose thrashed to regain his feet. Relief finally descended when the moose stood up only to fall again, one leg crumpled beneath it, the other across Big Hand's chest as if in an embrace. The Indian felt the warmth of "Yapi-moswak," (moose) on his cheek and the rise and fall of the great chest as the animal labored to sustain life. The spirit of the moose was that of strength and wisdom. Big Hand's unwavering faith in the spirit of the moose that he be treated with respect and kindness and not left to suffer prompted him to put the noble beast out of its misery. One quick pass with his hunting knife across he neck of the beast sent "Yapi-moswak" to Green Grass World, "Kihcikisik, (Heaven).

Exacerbated by the sub-arctic air, pain began to spread into Big Hand's shoulder and back. Realizing that he could not survive the relentless cold as he lay exposed to the harsh elements, the warrior thanked "Yapi-moswak" as he tore the insides from the lifeless moose and crawled inside its cavity for warmth and shelter. From within the noble beast, the trapper watched the entrails form a billowing cloud of steam, wisp away into the frigid air to the scavengers that feast on the dead, as well as the hunters seeking their prey. The raven and timber wolf were drawn to the scent of blood, and they circled the captive man and moose. Each time the wolves would venture too near their would-be feast, Big Hand would call on "Chuetenshu" (North Wind), the creator of animals, for aid and would then fire the Henry to scare the wolves away. His bullets spent, the warrior then grasped his knife in blood-covered hand and recited a prayer to Kice-Manito. In his struggles to keep the hungry wolves at bay and the pain that wracked his injured body in check, Big Hand thought longingly of the Great Creator, his wife, and daughter, Little Deer That Runs. As the warmth gradually fled from his body, Big Hand heard a rifle report. Using all the strength left inside him, he hollered, "Wichihin!"

It was Pierre who broke the ice that entombed Big Hand and laid him gently on the toboggan. The younger trapper carefully removed his own buffalo robe and covered the half-frozen body of his elder. It was a struggle to pull the furs and the injured trapper 300 feet to where Pierre had left his labors. Thinking quickly, Pierre dug a hole through the thick crust of snow and stashed both his furs and those of Big Hand. Pierre then covered the site with a toboggan and branches to protect their furs from the scavengers until he could retrieve them later on. As Pierre pulled Big Hand the three miles to his homestead, he wondered if his passenger was a live man or a corpse. When he reached the beaver pond where he had tied the tobacco pouch to the story pole, he stopped long enough to retrieve his feigned gratuity. He was a bit surprised to find life still in the old man's body when they finally reached home. The only sign of life at that were short gasps of breath that came moments apart.

It took three days of forcing warm pemmican soup and water down Big Hand's throat before the trapper regained consciousness. Pierre had just about given up hope of his patient's survival and was contemplating retrieving the furs he had stashed up river. Early that morning he began to ready himself for the task. He was about to leave the wigwam when he heard a faint voice.

"Wichinin Nimanitom," (Help me, my God.), and saw a hand raise from the blanket. Pierre's respect for the sanctity of life compelled him to return his attention to his unwelcome guest. He spent the rest of the day caring for Big Hand and watching his remarkable recovery. Kice-Manito had indeed heard Big Hand's prayer. Throughout the night, Pierre nursed his patient. Each time Big Hand awakened, he became more lucid so that by morning he had revived enough to make a request of the French trapper.

"Please go to my village and tell them where I am."

Pierre was more than happy to do Big Hand's bidding. He was eager to retrieve the pelts that he had buried up river. Pierre was only about one mile from his homestead when he met Ed DeGrace and two other men from Big Hand's village. They had left the village to search for Big Hand who was long overdue from his expected return from his trap line. Ed went with Pierre to secure the furs and left Big Hand with his friends to return the trapper to his family. It was a good opportunity for Ed DeGrace to convey to Pierre the quality, morality, and honor of the man whose life he had saved. After Ed harvested Big Hand's trap line, he relinquished it to Pierre for the rest of the season.

Little Deer That Runs heard the story of her father's ordeal from both Big Hand and Ed Degrace. She immediately wanted to go to the man who had saved her father's life and tell him how much she appreciated what he had done; however, her responsibilities kept her in the village while the snow was on the ground. A young girl's romantic fantasy captured Little Deer That Runs' imagination that winter. As Big Hand's health improved, so did Little Deer That Runs' admiration progress for the mysterious Frenchman she had never met. The maid devoted every spare minute that winter to sewing the finest moose skin shirt and leggings she had ever made. Her father, too, wanted to show his appreciation to Pierre for coming to his rescue, but it was hard for him to let go of the animosity he felt for a white man claiming land so close to his village. Knowing that Kisi-Manito wanted all peoples to love one another caused great conflict within Big Hand. Since the trapper had been chosen by his village long ago to be the leader of hunting parties, Big Hand, to show gratitude to Pierre, decided to invite his rescuer to accompany him on the early spring hunt. Suspecting her father's intentions, Little Deer That Runs insisted on going along. She let her imagination wander as she pictured herself handing her would-be lover the decorated shirt and leggings now wrapped in a soft beaver skin blanket. How their eyes would meet as he touched her hand and his heart would be filled with love for her.

While Little Deer That Runs fantasized meeting the man of her dreams, one of the braves on the hunting part, an ardent admirer of her, followed the maid around at every opportunity to show his interest.

Little Deer's overzealous praise of Pierre in the brave's presence was designed to fend off the latter's advances, but the end result was jealousy and resentment toward Pierre. Pierre's rival, Tall Tree (Ka Kinwackosit Mito) was influential among the young men in his village and well known for his hunting skills and quick temper. He, too, was looking forward to meeting Pierre as was Little Deer That Runs, but for entirely different reasons.

When the hunting party arrived at Pierre's homestead, he was busy constructing the log cabin that he was hoping to move into before the winter snows. As before, he stood with his pipe in his outstretched hand, observing Big Hand approach on an Indian pony. Little Deer That Runs and Ed DeGrace accompanied the elder warrior, the two of them sitting astride horses with travois behind them. Tall Tree and another brave were on foot. As the party stood before Pierre, the young trapper found it difficult to keep his eyes off Little Deer That Runs. Out of respect and acknowledgement that Big Hand was the leader of the group, Pierre tried to keep his eyes focused upon the older man, but with little success. Each time his eyes were drawn to the beautiful young girl, he captured her enticing smile. No sooner had the formal greetings been exchanged than Little Deer That Runs hurried to the travois and retrieved her gift for Pierre. When she handed Pierre the bundle, she laid her hand upon his and gently held it there for an instant. Their eyes met, and it was obvious to Pierre and everyone present that the beautiful maiden was smitten by the handsome French trapper. It was especially obvious to Tall Tree, a would-be suitor, who would later cause considerable difficulties in the courtship of Pierre and Little Deer That Runs.

When Lynes awakened, he could hear the current lapping at the riverbank and the mournful call of the loon. He did not wish to open his eyes to see where the party was camped. The site was torn up ground, covered mostly with rotting bark and mud holes. All the trees were logged off right up to the riverbank with the exception of those that were unmarketable. The landing on which they were camped was the only place where they could get near the river itself. Everywhere else was overlaid with brush, tangled branches and discarded treetops, all barring any access to the river. If he kept his eyes tightly shut, Pierre could smell the freshness of the water in a gentle breeze that swept the stream. Cheval's nicker reminded him that it was time to perform his first chore of the day. The horse fed and a quick breakfast eaten, the group set out on the last leg of their journey.

As the wagon rumbled down the deep-rutted and frequently muddy trail, Lynes noted the wheat fields and cornfields, the likes of which he had never seen. The Prince Albert Lumber Company was operating at full steam, apparently, as Lynes detected a large column of smoke rising from their burner, cumulating in a huge black cloud slowly drifting to the east. Log booms (a series of logs chained together to encircle and contain logs waiting to be processed), lined the east bank of the North Saskatchewan River. As the men stood on the west bank of the river, waiting for the ferry to transport them into Prince Albert, Ed Degrace was wondering if anyone would recognize him from the days when he fought against the Dominion. He conjectured that he might be wanted by the Northwest Mounted Police, and Prince Albert was its headquarters in Saskatchewan. Already, several of Ed's compatriots had been hanged or imprisoned, and he had no desire to join one or the other group.

When Cheval stepped off the ferry, Lynes entered a strange new world. Prince Albert had been designated a city just three years earlier, and at that time, was the capital of Saskatchewan. The transcontinental railway had arrived in the city, and it was assumed that it would continue from there to Edmonton, Alberta, Canada. That achievement would make Prince Albert the railhead for the province of Saskatchewan. In anticipation of that event, a group of wealthy investors from the East Coast opened a sawmill on the banks of the North Saskatchewan whereby they employed around 2,000 men to log the timber and work in the mill.

The city proper was the picture of success and prosperity. The busy streets were crowded with fashionable ladies in wide-brimmed hats made with exotic feathers, which kept swirling and swooping around their heads. Men wearing bowlers and high button shoes as well as working men in denims, and Indians and trappers in leather breeches hurried along the street. Buckboards, freight wagons, and surreys occupied River Street along with two of the most amazing contraptions

Lynes had ever seen. The objects were moving down the street toward him, smoke belching from behind, making a strange rattling noise that spooked the horses as they rolled past. Lynes's steed showed his displeasure with the horseless carriages by crow hopping and getting his leg tangled in the tugs. Lynes was hoping he would get a chance to examine one of these unusual vehicles before he left Prince Albert.

The sunset was just a dim glow on the horizon when the crew finished unloading and grading the furs at the Hudson Bay Company. Lynes dropped Cheval off at the livery stable then joined the others in bedding down at the Prince Albert Hotel on Central Avenue. With all the excitement of the day, Lynes found it hard to go to sleep that night. Footsteps in the hallway, closing doors, sounds of passing wagons on the street below, the faint jangle of music from the Nickelodeon in the hotel lobby, and an occasional loud voice from the active street, all kept Lynes awake well into the night. He was still ingesting the pulse of civilization when he heard the whistle from the sawmill announcing the midnight changing of the shifts. He likened the noise to the scream of a mountain lion shattering the familiar night sounds of the wilderness.

When the groggy boy stepped out of the hotel, he paused for a few minutes, searching up and down the street, trying to decide which direction to take. There was so much he wanted to see, and this would be his only full day in the city. Luckily, the whistle from the train directed his feet toward the railroad tracks and Broadway. Lynes strolled slowly down Central Avenue, stopping every now and then to study his surroundings and the bustling people as they passed by. He would look into the eyes of each person he passed and nod his head as an acknowledgement of their presence, a natural and courteous custom in a Cree village or on the rustic trail. He learned quickly that most of the men in high button shoes, and women in feathery hats, were not aware of the customs of the wilderness. There was a fleeting encounter with a young woman during his explorations that had aroused a sensation he had never before experienced. The young woman, wearing a high-necked dress that nearly touched the ground, was walking toward him. The color of the dress was the blue of a robin's egg. A snow-white apron accented the dress, as did the lacy pink ribbon worn around the girl's tiny waist. Her hair was swept in waves high on her head with golden curls flowing over her shoulders. Each step closer revealed even more of her beauty. Lynes stood still, waiting for her to pass. When she arrived within a few steps of him, he gazed into her eyes and gave her his nod of courtesy. To the stricken boy, it seemed as if he were looking into deep pools of sparkling blue water that exuded happiness and love. Lynes was engulfed in her beauty. His Isolde slowed her steps, and for what seemed like an eternity, held him in her eyes. The loveliest lips he had ever seen formed a smile, and a gentle voice said, "Bonjour," as she continued on her way. Lynes twisted his body to watch her walk away as he felt a sudden warmth, deep within his chest. He had for just an instant touched the life of the most enchanting creature on the earth. The sudden warmth grew into a consuming fire when the person under observation hesitated before entering the hotel and looked back at Lynes. With her arm at her side, her soft white hand gave a subtle wave in his direction. Lynes wanted to run back to the hotel, but he rationalized that the lovely girl lived in a different world from his, and like witnessing the ghostly beauty of the Northern Lights, he must content himself with the privilege of beholding a beautiful apparition beyond his reach.

It was disturbing for Lynes to get the image of the girl in the blue dress out of his mind as he ambled along Broadway peering into the shop windows. Pierre had given him $5.00, and he was shopping for gifts that he could take back to the homestead for his mother, brother, and sister. While he was searching for the right gifts, Lynes spotted a poster hanging in one of the show windows. The Prince Albert Lumber Company it seemed was looking to hire men to haul supplies into the lumber camps up the North Saskatchewan River and its tributaries. A long, hard, and dangerous trip could only be accomplished in the dead of winter when the river was frozen solid. The poster read, 'Only those with survival experience in the winter wilderness need apply.' No one met those qualifications better than Lynes. Wages for the season were promised to be twice as much as a fur trapper could make, but to the boy, the money was not the only consideration. This was the opportunity Lynes had been looking for. He cherished the time he spent with his father, but an inexplicable occurrence happened that winter that prompted Lynes to dread the upcoming trapping season.

Pierre was retrieving a beaver from a trap at a beaver lodge while Lynes went down a game trail where they had formerly set a box trap for small game. When Lynes brushed the fresh fallen snow from the box, two small black eyes peered up at him from within a pure white ball of fluff. A little black button nose like that on a child's stuffed toy protruded from the fur that was whiter than snow. This creature was not the first arctic fox that Lynes had ever killed, but it was the first wild animal that touched his soul. Each blow with the killing club that winter sent a pain throughout his body and left him feeling as if he were destroying a part of himself and the world. There was no way he could explain to his father, Pierre, why or how his feelings evolved. He did not understand it himself. Lynes wondered if he had been touched by "Chuetenshu," who was the lord of the animals in his mother's religion.

One of the feats Lynes was determined to do in Prince Albert was to get close enough to the locomotive to touch it, He recalled three years earlier when he first saw the powerful engine that appeared like a monstrous contraption with a life of its own. Black smoke bellowed from its stack, and it appeared to be coughing as Lynes cautiously approached it. Without warning, the iron beast gave a violent cough and an ear-splitting scream as Lynes became engulfed in steam. He had never experienced such a fright. Now, as he stood once again scrutinizing the locomotive, he reflected upon how his silly fears. For three years, he longed to touch the powerful engine to prove to himself that he wasn't afraid of it. Reconciled to the fact that it was just a piece of machinery, Lynes started to walk away, but then he turned and gingerly touched the locomotive anyway. Having accomplished his major mission in Prince Albert, the young Frenchman continued on his sightseeing tour of the city. After buying brightly colored ribbons and cloth for his mother and sister, and a bone-handled knife for Oliver, Lynes headed back to the hotel to wrap his gifts. After all, it was well into the afternoon and there was still much of the downtown district that Lynes wished to explore. The thriving city had almost doubled in size since his last visit.

On the way back to the hotel, Lynes noticed Ed DeGrace's horse tied to the hitching post in front of the North Star Tobacco and Apothecary. When Lynes walked through the door, his blood ran cold. Two Northwest Mounted Police were talking to his friend. Lynes remembered how Ed had been concerned that he might be recognized as one of Riel's patriots. When Ed's and Lynes's eyes met, Lynes caught the quick eye movement that signaled him to get out of there. Reluctant to leave Ed, Lynes strode over to where the men were talking as if he were browsing. He was close enough to overhear that the Mounties were going to take Ed into custody. It was obvious to the Mounties that Ed had been living with the Indians for a long time by his attire--the buckskins, moccasins, and long braided hair. Men who were trying to avoid the authorities commonly sought refuge with the natives. Ed explained to the Red Coats that he had been living with the Shoshones on the Yellowstone; he did not want to draw attention to the Cree village on the Little Red River. It could be that the authorities also wanted Big Hand. The Mounties' motto that, 'They always get their man,' included anyone who had fought against them in the Northwest Rebellion.

Lynes left the tobacco shop and untied Ed's horse from the hitching post. He thought perhaps his friend would make a break for it and elude the Mounties. However, Ed stumbled out of the shop in handcuffs, and the Mounties led him down the street toward their headquarters. Lynes was devastated; Ed had been Pierre's closest friend and was considered as part of the Duchneaux family. Feeling helpless and confused, Lynes mounted Ed's horse and headed for the hotel, all the while hoping his father would be there when he arrived. In his youthful innocence, Lynes thought that if his father went to the Mounties and told them what a good man Ed really was, the officers would let their friend go. On the way to the hotel, Lynes saw Pierre walk out of B. C. Seale Real Estate Broker's office. He could feel his heart start to hammer away inside his chest as he related to Pierre what had just happened. Pierre closed his eyes and lowered his head for about four seconds, an action Lynes had observed his father doing on previous occasions. The behavior occurred when Pierre found himself in an untenable situation. Lynes often wondered if his father was asking God for help or if he was just collecting his thoughts. Either way, Pierre would usually devise a plan of action. Lynes had acquired the same habit, but more often than not when he closed his own eyes and lowered his head, three words would enter his mind, "Guide me, Father."

Although Lynes's religion was a bit convoluted, he was a very spiritual person. In his early years, much of what Lynes learned was from his mother, Margarette, who, like her own father, took the Cree religion very seriously. After the boy learned to read and write in English and French, the Holy Bible was his textbook, and the Jesuit missionaries who taught him took God and Jesus quite seriously. Lynes had no difficulty reconciling the two religions--the Cree and the Catholic faiths. From his earliest memory, Lynes was constantly translating the First Nations language into French or into English and vice versa. To Lynes, Kice-Manito, translated to God; Kimanitominaw to Jesus; Machi Manito to the devil; Manito to the angels; Askitci to heaven; and Machimanitonahk to hell. Lynes learned how to pray in missionary school, but he felt more comfortable praying to God in his mother's fashion. When Pierre bowed his head, Lynes pictured the tall cathedral he had seen earlier when he left the hotel. He thought that now would be a good time to go to that holy place and pray for his friend, Ed DeGrace. There was little doubt in his trusting mind that this was a time for prayer.

Pierre raised his head and with an angry look on his face sternly stated, "I'll take care of this; wait for me at the hotel." And almost at a run, the trapper headed in the direction of the Mounties' headquarters.

Sergeant Major P. Marshall sat at his desk. Marshall had been sent West in the newly formed Northwest Mounted Police 33 years earlier as a young recruit, to stop the white men from using whiskey to trade for furs with the First Nations' People. He never forgot what he was sent west for, but wasn't blind to the many forms of exploitation the Parliament and business interests were practicing. He had also been at the Battle of Frenchman's Butte and held the Indians and Riel's Patriots in contempt. Marshall had the authority to allow Pierre to visit Ed, but he denied the trapper's request until after Ed came before the judge and bail was set. Rejected and angry, Pierre strode from the building, determined to do everything within his power to free Ed from jail.

On his way back to the hotel, Lynes impulsively decided he would go to God's house and say a prayer on his friend's behalf. The newly constructed St. Paul's Presbyterian Church was a wonder to the innocent boy as he gazed upward at the tall brick bell tower. The boy was awestruck again when he cautiously entered the building. The beautiful oak interior and the Gothic style stained glass windows depicting Christ and his apostles gave Lynes a feeling of deep reverence. Alone, and in the silence of the vast space of the nave, Lynes felt he had indeed entered the house of the Lord. Although he felt more comfortable praying in Michif, this was a house the missionaries had built so he knelt down in front of the stained glass windows and began to pray in English as the missionaries had instructed him. From the tales Ed and Big Hand recounted about the aftermath of the Northwest Rebellion, Lynes was certain that Ed was destined for the gallows. The young trapper prayed earnestly, unaware of the tears rolling down his cheeks. He was entreating God to save his friend with such fervent intensity that he was oblivious to the physical world around him. He did not hear the footsteps come down the aisle nor see the beautiful young lady in a dress the color of a robin's egg, sit down in the pew nearest the stained glass window.

While Lynes prayed, his father contemplated on how he would free Ed from jail. Pierre's inclination was to march to the jail and break Ed out forcibly, but it was clear what that outcome would bring. Finally, after wrestling with his choices, Pierre realized that his only legitimate recourse would was to seek out a barrister. It was not without some trepidation that the trapper walked into the office of McKay and Adams, Barristers, Solicitors, and Advocates. Every visible evidence indicated that McKay and Adams was a very successful firm. The law office was centrally located in the downtown district. A discreet sign hung over glass paneled mahogany French doors. The foyer was decorated with solid oak carved wainscot that could be seen from the street through a large plate glass window. As Pierre waited nervously in the overstuffed chair next to the large receptionist's desk, he reckoned that he would soon be conversing with a barrister that had the contacts to benefit his friend. There was little doubt in Pierre's mind that the $25.00 (the equivalent of two prime beaver pelts) that he gave the receptionist for consultation was well spent.

The private office of James McKay proved even more impressive than the foyer. Behind the barrister's oversized oak desk and totally covering the back wall was a geographic map of Saskatchewan. Law books dominated an adjoining wall, while the opposite wall held a portrait of Wilfrid Laurier, the Prime Minister of Canada. Wilfrid Laurier was the first French-speaking Head of State in Canada, and he supported the establishment of a French-English Canada under the British Crown. The man was also famous for his speech supporting Riel after he had been captured and sentenced to be hanged. Diplomas from universities and other schools of higher learning surrounded the portrait. Pierre was confident that McKay was the best barrister that he could retain in Prince Albert. When the six-foot-six inch imposing figure stood up and reached across the desk to shake the trapper's hand, Pierre felt secure that this giant of a man was going to be the one person that could save his friend, Ed DeGrace.

Lynes was also seeking help in saving Ed DeGrace but from a different venue. He felt conflicted with utter exhaustion as he slowly recovered from a deep meditative state that had brought him inner peace. However, the passage of time had escaped Lynes so he felt it urgent to return to the hotel to meet his father. As he rose and turned, Lynes was startled by the presence of the beautiful girl in the blue dress. How long has she been sitting there? Does she see the dampness on my face and know that I've been crying? These and other questions flashed through Lynes's head as he stood dumbfounded, staring at the vision in front of him.

Her bright blue eyes widened as she tilted her head downward and gazed up at Lynes. She spoke in an almost timid voice, "I am sorry if I startled you, but as I sat here praying, I could not help but feel your sadness."

A long silence followed. Lynes searched for something coherent to say, but the girl's beauty and fragrance left him speechless.

"My name is Monique Renee; I come here each day to pray for the Lord's guidance. It always makes me feel good to sense his love. Would you like me to pray with you? Perhaps it would make you feel better, too?" She held out her hand to Lynes.

Lynes's initial urge to flee was suppressed by the magical charm of Monique's countenance. He had no way of knowing that her "Bonjour" and pretty smile earlier in the day was because of her attraction to him. Monique was stirred with excitement at Lynes's attention when they passed each other on the street. She thought what a thrill it would be to be pursued by such a ruggedly handsome backwoodsman. She had just entered her sixteenth year and was quite aware of her sexuality. Although Monique was seldom out of her governess's sight, the added attention she was receiving from young men made it conspicuously clear that she had blossomed into a desirable young woman. Monique was born into an aristocratic family from Quebec whose father, Robert Tredeaux, held considerable influence with the French-speaking, liberal citizens in the provinces. However Monique admired her father, he used his political skills and influence behind the scenes to support whichever candidate benefited his financial interests. Currently, he was in Prince Albert to gain support for the newly formed Provincial Rights Party led by Frederick Haultain. The latter was also a member of the gentility.

This was the first time Monique had ever ventured beyond the shielded life of the wellborn. She felt free from restraints in this newly formed province. The young girl relished the danger, excitement, and independence for which the new province was noted. To Lynes, Monique's voice sounded like a choir of angels. He wondered if she would understand Michif (a language from the descendants of French fur trappers and their Cree Indian wives). Monique was bewildered when Lynes took her hand. His face was stern, almost as if he were angry, but he spoke softly in Michif. He spoke as he would to a fawn and its mother so as not to cause them fear. "You are the most beautiful creature I have ever seen. I am sorry that I have to leave so soon."

He knew she would not understand what he said, or he wouldn't have been quite so bold. When he finished speaking, he released Monique's soft, warm hand and reluctantly walked away. As Lynes left the church, he struggled to erase the ecstasy of the moment. His mind was once again plagued with the events of the day and concern that Pierre would be waiting impatiently for him at the hotel.

When James McKay introduced himself to Pierre, he was upset that his receptionist had permitted a simple trapper to take up his valuable time. The barrister represented the Imperial Bank of Canada, the Hudson Bay Company, and many of the wealthy politicians who were gaining control of the land and resources in the newly formed Province of Saskatchewan. One of his sidelines was real estate. Up until this year, Saskatchewan had been the Wild, Wild West for lawyers, and James McKay was packing the biggest gun. He had been appointed King's Council and was now opposing the very man whose portrait he sported on his wall. James McKay was amusing himself as he listened to Pierre painfully explain his friend's dilemma. Pierre was unaware that McKay supported the government's policy of cultural genocide of the Indians and the Metis peoples, and had fought in the militia against Riel twelve years earlier. With a sly grin on his face, the lawyer told Pierre that he was going to take care of Ed DeGrace. When Pierre left the office, McKay picked up the telephone and asked to be connected to the Northwest Mounted Police Headquarters.

On the way to the hotel, Pierre saw Ed's horse standing in front of Saint Paul's Presbyterian Church. At first, he was agitated that Lynes had not gone straight to the hotel as he had instructed, but when he entered the church and saw Lynes on his knees in front of the figure of Jesus, there was a tug at his heart. He quietly closed the door to the sanctuary and then left a scribbled note on the horse's saddle, instructing Lynes to take Ed's horse to the livery stable and then go straight back to the hotel.

Lynes walked into their hotel room where he saw Pierre sitting on the edge of his bed, elbows on his knees and his chin resting upon his fists. He sat down in a chair near the window and waited for his father to say something.

"Well, son, it looks like our trip back home is going to be postponed for a while. The bastards have Ed locked up, and I won't be able to see him until tomorrow morning."

Pierre continued on, telling Lynes about the top-notch lawyer he had acquired to defend their friend. When Pierre mentioned how much the lawyer was going to cost, it gave Lynes an opening to suggest to his father that he might be able to haul freight that winter to make up for the exorbitant attorney fees. Lynes didn't know that when he saw his father step out of B. C. Seal Real Estate Broker's office, that he had been negotiating to sell the homestead. Pierre did not intend to run his trap lines that winter. While Lynes had been sightseeing, Pierre had been loading the wagon with supplies and materials to update the homestead and ready it as advertised. Without Ed, Pierre was doubtful that his plans could be completed. Ed had always played a big role in the development and success of the homestead. In fact, without Ed, there might never have been the Dashneaux family unit. Ed, then, was the topic of conversation that long, anxious night. It was inevitable that Pierre would tell Lynes, for the first time, how Ed made it possible for him to capture the hand of Little Deer That Runs. Dutifully, Lynes listened intently as his father related the events of that courtship.

"When Little Deer That Runs gave me the buckskin shirt and leggings, I was flattered by her attention and the many gifts that other visitors brought, the most valuable of which was a large eight-month-old dog. The little dog had already proven himself to be the alpha canine among the younger dogs in the village and was fully trained to pull a travois. Big Hand then proudly presented me the rawhide leash saying, 'His name is Pihesiwak (Thunder).'

"To show his appreciation, Pierre went into his wigwam and strolled out with a large pouch of tobacco and a colorful string of beads. He presented the tobacco to Big Hand and the beads to his admirer. Pierre's experience on the Yellowstone had taught him that keeping well-stocked in tobacco, beads, and whiskey would hold him in good stead with the First Nations people. Although he knew it was against the law to give whiskey to the Indians, he brought out a small quantity, just enough to keep the Indians there for the evening. Pierre was glad to see his old friend again and relished the attention given to him by Little Deer That Runs. Pierre pulled some recently killed deer from his cache, and Little Deer That Runs accepted the meat, eager to show Pierre her culinary skills.

"With the exception of Tall Tree, everyone was enjoying Pierre's hospitality. By the end of the day, Big Hand had dispelled any doubts as to the veracity of Pierre. The father was even able to tolerate his pride and joy's flirting gestures toward the young French trapper. On the other hand, Tall Tree did everything possible, short of confronting Big Hand, to show his own intentions regarding his desire for Little Deer That Runs' affections. It was customary among the First Nations people that the father of the man in question give a gift to the man who courted his daughter, but only if he deemed the man worthy. The gift was usually a horse. When Big Hand gave Thunder to Pierre, Ed

DeGrace was not surprised to note a guarded display of anger from Tall Tree, the gift of the dog, being an intrinsic and valuable part of the Woodland Cree. That gift kindled Tall Tree's jealousy.

"When the shadows fell over the meadow and the cold late spring mist began to settle, Pierre invited the band to spend the night inside his wigwam. The first to enter the shelter was Little Deer That Runs who was quick to place her robe next to where Pierre's bed was prepared. When Tall Tree tried to lay his robe next to Little Deer That Runs, Big Hand told the brave that was where he was going to sleep. Careful not to show his anger to Big Hand, Tall Tree moved his robe to the other side of the wigwam. The customary sleeping arrangement of the First Native peoples was not adhered to that night.

"Pierre was accustomed to the solitary silence of the wilderness. The sound of breathing surrounded him, and he found it hard to go to sleep. The presence of Little Deer That Runs lying so close to him aroused his manhood, and when he turned to look at her, she was gazing at him with a seductive look on her face. This was not the time nor the place. Pierre rolled over and pretended to go to sleep. Well into the night as Pierre lay sleepless, he felt something touch his robe. It was Little Deer That Runs. Through the entrance of the wigwam, Pierre watched the full moon transform the meadow into a silver cloud as the evening mist rolled in. The mating call of the timber wolf rang out in the distance. Thunder raised his head and let out a low growl.

"In the morning, the hunt went well. Pierre had already scouted out his next hunt and guided the hunting party to a small lake with an abundance of water lillies and pondweed, both staples in the moose diet. The lake was surrounded by white birch another favorite of the moose. Before the sun took the chill out of the morning air, the travois' were loaded with moose, and the hunting party was headed back to Little Red River village. Pierre had proved himself to Big Hand and had hinted that, "Any man would be honored to be the husband of Little Deer hat Runs."

"It was two days after the hunt that Ed became concerned about the safety of Pierre. He overheard two of Tall Tree's close friends talking about how much Tall Tree suggested they would profit by eliminating his competition. Ed had observed Tall Tree grow up and was fully aware of his inclination to violence and also his cunning in hiding his wrongdoing. In fact, the trapper had caught the brave in lies and deceit several times over the years. Tall Tree, in turn, realized that Ed recognized his deceptiveness, and so the brave avoided Ed because of the trapper's close friendship with Big Hand. However, through his quick wit and talent for diplomacy, Tall Tree had gained considerable prominence within the community and the collective confidence of the village. Ed knew he would have a hard time convincing the Council that the brave was plotting to do away with Pierre, his rival. Reluctantly, Ed approached Big Hand, hoping to defuse the growing conflict. The trapper was careful not to accuse Tall Tree of plotting against Pierre as the brave would just deny the accusation and put Ed himself in a bad light with Big Hand. After all, it was Big Hand who had chosen the sacred place where Tall Tree took his Vision Quest; it was the warrior who gave the brave his instructions for his rite of passage from childhood to manhood. With all these considerations in mind, Ed approached Big Hand.

"Mon ami, I am worried for Tall Tree. I think he is jealous of Pierre and might do something stupid."

"Big Hand hesitated before he spoke. "No, he gets angry, but he has a good spirit. He is just young and in heat. He will get over it." Tall Tree had always put on his best face when he was around Big Hand.

"Why haven't you chosen him? You know that he is in love with Little Deer That Runs."

"I know he is, but he will have to go on more than one Vision Quest before he is worthy of my little girl."

Ed laughed and put his hand on Big Hand's shoulder. "It'll take one hell of a man to be worthy of Little Deer That Runs."

Big Hand laughed, "You betcha!"

"When Ed left the warrior, he wasn't sure if their short conversation had served its purpose, but he was sure of one thing--he was going to keep an eye on Tall Tree and his two cohorts. The next day Ed left the village to warn Pierre. The urgency in Ed's voice convinced Pierre that he was indeed in danger. To be on the safe side, Pierre built a concealed shelter near his wigwam to insure his safety at night.

"A few days after Ed's visit to Pierre, the trapper began to notice strange behavior around Tall Tree's wigwam. Kimapahkew (He Who Watches On The Sly) and Wasakapahtaw (Runs In A Circle) seldom left Tall Tree's side. These two were the braves that Ed had overheard discussing Tall Tree's competition. All three young braves left the village, and Tall Tree as usual was carrying his Springfield musket. A cougar's claw necklace hung from the stock. The cougar claws were Tall Tree's talisman, and he would not allow anyone to touch his musket. Just minutes later, Ed was surprised to see Kimapahkew holding Tall Tree's musket. Tall Tree was instructing Kimapahkew how to quickly load and fire the gun. Over the course of the week, Ed observed the same type of instructions being given to Tall Tree's friends. Alert to impending mischief, Ed continued his vigilance that paid off when, in the middle of the night, a village dog let out a quiet "woof" from near Tall Tree's wigwam, indicating some movement in the village. Ed watched Tall Tree stealthily creep from the village, carrying his Springfield. (Tall Tree never left the village without his musket.) Ed was just about to follow the brave when Tall Tree walked back into the village, but he wasn't carrying his rifle. No sooner had Tall Tree entered his own wigwam than He Who Watches On The Sly, and Runs In A Circle crept silently out of the village and disappeared in the direction from which Tall Tree had returned minutes before. This was the moment that Ed was waiting for. The adrenaline began to rush through his body as it had at Duck Lake when the first shot was fired. Ed quietly awakened Big Hand.

"Mon ami, (Ed always addressed Big Hand and no one else as 'My Friend.') Forgive me for disturbing your sleep; I think Pierre is in danger and I need your help."

Big Hand rubbed his eyes and looked quizzically at Ed, "What makes you think he's in danger?"

"I overheard He Who Watches On The Sly and Runs In A circle discuss getting rid of someone. I wasn't sure of whom they were talking, but I just saw them sneaking out of the village, heading in the direction of Pierre's place. I hope I'm wrong, but I've a bad feeling."

"I hope you're wrong, too."

As Big Hand was getting ready to go with Ed, Walks On Water woke up. Big Hand assured her that everything was all right. "Go back to sleep; I'm going hunting."

"The moon was just a splinter as it moved across the sky, barely discernable in the star-studded heavens. When Big Hand and Ed left the wigwam, they were met with the brightness of a multitude of dazzling bodies that cast a faint light on the village clearing. As they entered the woods, they were cloaked in almost total darkness. Big Hand led the way, his footsteps steady and sure. Each step hardly left a sound as his moccasins slowly compressed whatever lay beneath them. If a tree branch or bush were in his path, one continuous motion of his hand and it was deftly moved aside and returned to its former place as if he had never passed that way. Like a nighthawk in the blackness of night, Big Hand made his way; Ed followed close behind, wondering, "How in the hell does he do that?"

"As each star faded in the morning light, Big Hand's pace increased. The Morning Star was all that remained in the sky when the warrior halted. He turned to Ed and signaled for silenced. They were nearing the meadow where Pierre lived, and Big Hand detected signs that someone or something was just minutes ahead. From that moment on and until the meadow and wigwam came into view, the two men crouched and moved forward like cats stalking their prey. Out of the stillness of the early morning, Big Hand heard a familiar sound--two loud barks that the warrior recognized as warning barks from Thunder. Big Hand smiled at Ed and whispered, "Pihesiwak," as the dog trotted into view. Big Hand looked in the direction that had aroused Thunder's attention and observed a slight movement in the brush about 200 feet from the wigwam. Uneasy that Pierre would dash out of his wigwam and be ambushed, Big Hand rose up and fired into the brush where he had seen the movement earlier. He hollered out, "Pierre, this is your friend! You are in danger! Be careful!"

"Those words were no more than shouted when Ed ran across the meadow in hot pursuit. A cloud of smoke appeared above the brush, and the crack of a musket ball whirred over the trapper's head. Another shot rang out, only this time it came from near the wigwam. Ed looked in the direction of the wigwam when he spied Pierre and Thunder as they raced toward the cloud of smoke still hanging in the air.

"Pierre had been sleeping in his concealed shelter, not the wigwam, when he was awakened by the growl coming from deep within Thunder's throat. His Henry in hand, the young trapper rolled out of his shelter and scanned for movement on the edge of the meadow. Two figures were detected just at the time he heard Big Hand's musket report. The intruders turned and began running. Pierre adroitly raised his Henry to his shoulder and squeezed the trigger. The two ambushers disappeared into the timber, followed closely by Pierre and Thunder. Big Hand and Ed DeGrace trailed behind.

"He Who Watches On The Sly came into view of his pursuers but was compelled to stop to reload the Springfield. Pierre raised his rifle to fire, but Big Hand pushed the barrel aside and screamed out, "Don't make me shoot you! Put that gun down!"

He Who Watches On The Sly continued loading the musket. Big Hand screamed another warning, "Don't do it!"

"The determined assailant finished loading and raised the musket to his shoulder. Big Hand fired. The 44-caliber slug slammed into the brave's side, spinning him like a top, and knocked him to the ground. When the two comrades stood stood looking down at their wounded friend, he screamed out in anguish, "Shoot me! Kill me!"

Tears welled in Big Hands' eyes. "Why! Why! Child. Why did you make me shoot you?"

"Kill me! There's nothing left for me. Kill me!"

"He Who Watches On The Sly was in anguish and did not want to face his family with the shame of what he tried to do. It was clear to Ed and Pierre as they watched Big Hand holding the young man in his arms that the warrior did not want him to die.

"You will live, Child, you will live. Why did you want to hurt another human being?" Big Hand spied Tall Tree's Springfield. "What are you doing with Tall Tree's musket?"

"Between groans He Who Watches On The Sly told Big Hand of Tall Tree's promise of wealth and favor if his friend did away with Pierre. Big Hand looked solemnly into Kimapahkew's eyes. "Witiko (an evil spirit) has taken you over."

"As Big Hand held Kimapahkew, Ed and Pierre treated the young Indian's wound. When the men tied the injured brave onto the travois to transport him back to the village, the brave was still begging them to put him out of his misery. He Who Watches On The Sly knew what the punishment would be when he returned, and worst of all, he would have to face Tall Tree." Having finished his tale, Pierre nodded off to sleep as did his son, Lynes.

Prince Albert was awakening when Lynes and Pierre left the hotel. The mill whistle was calling the day shift to work, and the rattle of harnesses and wagons filled the street. Pierre headed for the Mounted Police Headquarters, and Lynes headed for the livery stable to get Cheval and a teammate Pierre had purchased earlier. It would take a team to pull the load of materials Pierre acquired for the homestead.

Sergeant Marshall was at his desk and recognized Pierre when he strode into the office. "You must know somebody. I guess you get to see him before the judge does. He's in the jail a couple blocks from here."

Pierre didn't say anything but was patting himself upon his back for choosing an attorney with influence. When he stepped past the solid iron door into the cellblock, he was gripped with the dark, dank atmosphere surrounding him. Pierre thought of how Ed must have been struck with a feeling of hopelessness and despair when that iron door slammed shut behind him. Pierre hoped the assurance of a top-notch lawyer would give his friend some relief. Ed had a big smile on his face, but his eyes told a different story when he saw Pierre, "What the hell are you doing here?"

Pierre forced a smile and out of character, answered, "Just passing by and thought I'd stop by and say hello! No, I wanted to let you know that I got the best damn lawyer in Saskatchewan to get you out of here."

"Don't worry partenaire, (partner), I don't think they know who I am. I told them, 'I'm Ed Robinette from the Shoshone and just came up here to get in on the fur trade. Unless I run into a Mountie who knew me at Fort Pitt, I'll be OK. They arrested me because I had a gallon of whiskey with me. They think I'm a whiskey trader." Ed gave out a husky laugh.

Pierre was speechless. His thoughts flashed back to the night before and his conversation with Sergeant Marshall.

"What can I do for you?"

"I came in here to see my friend."

"What's your friend's name?"

"Ed DeGrace."

"We don't have an Ed DeGrace."

"You just arrested him no more than twenty minutes ago."

Pierre had the sinking feeling that he was responsible for his best friend's imminent destruction. Not only had he given Sgt. Marshall Ed's identity, but McKay as well. It cut like a knife in his heart to tell Ed of his blunder. At first, Pierre saw a look of astonishment and trouble on Ed's face, but as he continued on, the look of astonishment and trouble turned into total resignation.

"Oh well! What the hell! At least now I will know for sure if any of my old comrades gave the bastards my name before they went to jail."

Pierre and Ed visited until the turnkey, Peter Forsyth, trudged in to inform them that visiting time was over. Pierre assured Ed that he would be back the next day to find out what time he would see the Judge. Ed's last words were, "Tell Lynes to take good care of my horse."

Cheval snorted and whinnied a welcome to Lynes when he walked up to the corral. In turn, Lynes gave him a handful of sugar cubes he had taken from a bowl on the counter at the hotel restaurant. The horse that his father bought was slightly smaller than Cheval and seemed to be well mannered as Lynes slipped the harness over his back. Prince and Cheval had become acquainted at the livery stable and worked well together. Lynes drove the pair the three miles to the Prince Albert mill where the wagon was partially loaded with lumber. After hooking up the team, Lynes pulled the wagon up to the general manager's office. A. L. Mattes, the general manager had just arrived from Minneapolis and wasn't fully up to speed on the hiring practices at the Prince Albert mill. Neither was Lynes. The boy walked boldly into Mattes' office to apply for the job he had seen on the poster. Most of the teamsters hauling freight in the winter were Indians who were well acquainted with the river systems and knew how to survive the hardships of the Saskatchewan winters. However, Mattes was impressed with the young trapper's sincerity and confidence. Lynes strutted out of the office with the teamster job in November and an offer for a job anytime he wanted it.

Pierre walked into Sgt. Major Marshall's office after he visited Ed. "Could you tell me when my friend is scheduled to see a judge?"

The Sergeant smiled, "Which friend? Ed Robinette or Ed DeGrace?"

"Both."

"Tomorrow at 1:30 PM."

Pierre left the Northwest Police Mounty headquarters feeling worse than he did when he had walked in. His next stop was at the law office of James McKay. The clerk didn't make the mistake of wasting McKay's time with a trapper again. He told Pierre that McKay was out, and he would see him at the arraignment tomorrow. Pierre had a feeling of impending disaster as he trudged back to the hotel to meet Lynes. His son had not yet returned to the hotel, and Pierre grew restless waiting in the room. He turned and walked downstairs to wait for Lynes in the lounge. There was only one patron in the lounge that early in the day and that one was nursing the results of the night before.

Alex Morrison welcomed Pierre into his haunt. Alex was a jovial middle-aged man who never met a man he didn't like, sober or drunk. Inquisitive to a fault and a consummate conversationalist, he had his finger on the pulse of Prince Albert. He was also quick to let anyone who would listen know it. After learning that Pierre was new in town, Alex was pleased to have an audience to whom he could tout the importance of Prince Albert. Pierre was deep in his own thoughts and was ignoring the floodgate of rhetoric flowing from Alex as he polished the glasses behind the bar and feigned being busy, all the time keeping within the earshot of Pierre. As Alex expounded upon the esteemed clientele that frequented his lounge, the name McKay caught Pierre's attention.

"Wait a minute. What did you say about McKay?"

"Gentleman Joe? I thought everybody knew Gentleman Joe. He fired the first shot that started the Northwest Rebellion."

"Is he related to McKay? The big shot lawyer downtown?" Pierre got that sick feeling he had when he realized he had blown Ed's cover earlier.

"Naw, but he fought for the Queen in the Northwest Rebellion, too, and before that he got a posse together and trapped that Cow Killer, Almighty Voice, for the Mounties. He's pretty famous too. In fact, I think he'll be running against Laurier for Prime Minister next year."

Pierre had heard enough. Alex was still yakking as Pierre left the lounge. A lot was going through Pierre's mind as he waited for Lynes, not the least of which was his lousy choice of lawyers. Pierre had not been aware that McKay had fought in the Northwest Rebellion against his friend Ed and had also been involved in the death of Almighty Voice. It was a story that was well known on the reservations in Saskatchewan.

Almighty Voice was only twenty-one years old when he killed a reservation cow to feed his brother's sick daughter although the First Nations people were not allowed to kill anything without the Indian agent's permission. Because of Almighty Voice's infraction, he was arrested and placed in jail. While the Indian was being held in jail, another building was being constructed behind the jail. The jailer informed the native that the building was a scaffolding to hang him. Consequently, Almighty Voice escaped that night. Later on when a Mountie and a scout tried to arrest the Indian, he shot and killed the Mountie. For a year, Almighty Voice avoided capture in spite of a $500 reward on his head. Inspector Allen's men eventually discovered the brave by accident and tried to arrest him. Both Allen and one other man were wounded so they called in reinforcements. A posse formed by McKay surrounded Almighty Voice and his braves and kept them contained until the Mounties appeared. Underestimating the resolve of Almighty Voice and his companions, the Mounties and posse charged the braves. The Indians killed two Mounties and wounded one civilian. That night, Almighty Voice appealed to the Mounties to send them some food because they had fought all day and were hungry. The Mounties in response brought in cannon and killed all three of the Indian braves.

There are many renditions of the story of Almight Voice and the stolen cow, but it is a trueism that whoever wins the war writes the history. McKay himself was one-quarter Indian and was proud to let everyone know that his Indian family name was Bear Skin. Whenever it was beneficial to the occasion, the lawyer referred to himself as

Chief. The name, Bear Skin, was handed down to McKay from his grandfather who worked for the Hudson Bay Company and married an Indian chief's daughter. Although McKay touted the fact that he was Metis, he was not sympathetic to the First Nations' people or the French Metis who did not cooperate with the Crown's attempt to commit cultural genocide. The barrister was also unsympathetic to the injustices regularly perpetrated upon the Metis. Authorities awarded McKay with positions of power throughout his lifetime because he adhered to the policies of the Crown and the demographics of the times. Pierre's concerns for his friend, Ed, were not without just cause.

When Lynes returned to the hotel, he was riding Ed's horse, Pique. Pique was a gift awarded to Ed by the Plains Cree tribe of Big Bear and Wandering Spirit. Wandering Spirit's daughter had escaped at the Battle of Loon Lake, along with Big Hand, Wild Goose, Ed, and two other members of the Plains Cree tribe. Two years later, Wandering Spirit's daughter, Pimohtewin-Simac (Walks Straight Up), reunited with her mother near the Montana border. One day, two young braves, leading a string of three young horses, rode into the Little Red River Village. The horses were gifts for Big Hand, Wild Goose, and Ed DeGrace from Wandering Spirit's wife because the men had protected her daughter. It was rumored that while all the warriors on the gallows with Wandering Spirit were singing their death song or cursing their murderers, Wandering Spirit was softly singing a love song to his bereaved wife.

Although Pique was not branded, he was obviously from the US Cavalry stock, a black Morgan with a white spot in the middle of his forehead, configured in the shape of a spade. The horse's powerful legs and broad neck and chest did not overshadow his quiet countenance. Almost fifteen hands, the beast was indeed a magnificent specimen, and Ed's pride and joy. When Lynes rode up to Pierre in front of the hotel, Pierre gave Lynes a stern look.

"How did you know that Ed is holding you responsible for Pique while he is in jail?"

Lynes reached out and scratched Pique between the ears. "He's in good hands, Dad." Caring for Pique was a responsibility that Lynes was more than happy to bear.

47

The remainder of the day was spent loading up the wagon with materials to take back to the homestead and the Indian band on the Little Red River. That evening, Lynes sat for hours by the nickelodeon in the hotel lobby, hoping the lovely Monique would happen by. His effort was not in vain. As he was about to call it a night, a group of well-dressed men entered the lobby. Monique accompanied the men, her golden hair swept high on her head in Gibson Girl fashion, and the pearl white gown of silk and lace accentuated her ample breasts and tiny waist. A string of pearls and gold adorned the high-necked blouse that was fashionable for the times. It struck Lynes that she looked much older than she did when he last held her hand. The group paused for a moment as the father and daughter spoke, both looking in Lynes's direction. James McKay, Fredrick Haultian, and James Pendergast continued into the lounge. Monique and her father parted from the group and approached Lynes who sensed an air of aggression and intimidation in the older man's stride.

Lynes's senses were correct. Robert Treadeaux addressed him in a tone of voice obviously meant to intimidate, "What is your name young man?" He looked scornfully at Lynes as he would a decaying carcass, showing his blatant disapproval.

"Lynes Dashneaux, sir." Lynes was taken aback by the animosity directed toward him and fought back his tendency to lash out in anger.

"And how did you come to know my daughter?"

"It was by chance that we met in God's house yesterday."

"Monique wishes to speak with you. I will be in the lounge for a short while. DO NOT leave the lobby!"

A light cloud of cigar and pipe smoke hovered against the ceiling, the smell of scented pipe tobacco lingering in the air. The odors overwhelmed the subtle fragrance of Monique that Lynes had experienced in the church the day before. As Monique sat down, Lynes edged closer, trying to get near enough to re-capture the essence that enveloped her. All anger left Lynes; the beauty before him engulfed his total being. His mounting desire for the girl was beyond anything he had ever felt, and the excitement of her presence left him speechless. While Lynes had sat in the lobby, the most that he hoped for was that he would catch a glimpse of her as she passed by. This occasion was more than he had anticipated.

"Please forgive my father. I don't know why he was so rude. Perhaps it is because he worries about me."

"It's all right; I understand. Your father said you wanted to speak with me?"

"I told my father that I met you in church and how distressed you were. I told him we prayed together." She waited for Lynes's correction, but he remained silent.

"When I saw you there, I asked Daddy if I could talk to you about our meeting yesterday. He seemed sympathetic last night when I first told him about you. I don't know why he was so angry tonight."

"He must have his reasons." Lynes wanted to say something clever or something to impress her, but his mind was fighting back the urge to reach out and kiss her warm red lips and stroke her golden hair. Monique could see the longing in his eyes.

"When I passed you on the street yesterday morning, you made me feel so happy. Then when I saw your sadness in church, it touched my heart. I wanted to help you in your time of sorrow."

Monique began to feel an emotional connection with Lynes that went beyond the curiosity that originally drew her to him. In that instant, her mind flashed back to the excitement of his touch as he held her hand. She could visualize his dark eyes and how they penetrated her very soul; she heard his voice as soothing as the call of the mourning dove. She now raised her eyebrows as she gazed into his eyes, an indication that she wanted him to speak.

"I was surprised to see you sitting there. I was hoping that I would see you again, but not under those previous circumstances."

"You seemed so sad; have you lost a loved one?"

"No. I was saying a prayer for a close friend of mine who was having a bad day."

"I hope your prayers will be answered."

"I'll know tomorrow."

For just a second Lynes was struck with the pain he felt for his beloved friend, Ed, but Monique's lovely voice drew him back to the enchantment of the moment. "My father is here on business. I take my evening prayers at five o'clock while he is attending his meetings. Will I be able to see you there?"

Lynes was elated that this beautiful girl wanted to be with him again. "I would like to see you again, but I can't say what tomorrow will bring." Lynes almost panicked at the thought that he might have to leave Prince Albert without seeing Monique just one more time.

"There is something I just HAVE to ask you," she said with a smile.

"I thought you were angry with me when you accepted my hand last night, but your voice was so soft and tender. What did you say?"

"I was not angry. I was trying to hide how I felt about my friend. I said that you were the most beautiful creature on earth."

Monique nodded a coquettish tilt to her head. "Then I guess I will see you tomorrow." They both broke into laughter.

As a little girl, Monique had read books and heard tales of the Canadian frontier. She was intrigued with the stories of the Indian wars and the men who braved the wilderness to bring fortune to her beloved country. England's worldwide promotion to settle the Prairie Providences at that time gave way to stories of adventure, wealth, and romance. To Monique, Lynes represented all of the above. As they chatted, there were long pauses when they shared their feelings and longings only with their eyes as they gazed into each other's souls. Their conversation was cut short when Mr. Treadeaux strode from the lounge. When he approached Lynes, he did not appear to be in any better mood than he was at their first meeting. He first looked at Lynes and then to Monique.

"Is everything all right?"

"Yes, Father, we had a very good conversation."

"Good! It's time for you to get your rest. I'll be up shortly to look in on you. I want to talk to your friend for a minute."

Monique turned to Lynes, "Goodnight, Lynes."

Hearing her voice say his name echoed through Lynes's brain as he watched, transfixed, as Monique disappeared up the stairs. He then turned to Mr. Treaudeaux. "Yes sir?"

"Young man, it should be obvious to you that my daughter does not fit into your social community. I don't know if her interest in you is out of sympathy or curiosity, but whatever it is, I DO NOT want you to pursue this relationship. Is that understood?"

Lynes looked quizzically at Monique's father. In Lynes's world, there had never been any social boundaries, and to Lynes, Monique's fondness for him was pure and genuine. He stood searching for an answer.

"Do you understand?" Treadeaux boomed.

"Yes, I understand that you fear for your daughter's safety. She is safe with me."

"Just stay away from my daughter!" Treaudeaux abruptly turned and stalked up the stairs.

Returning to the hotel, Lynes found his father gazing thoughtfully out the window. Pierre asked where he had been. It was obviously a rhetorical question, as other more pressing problems seemed to be on Pierre's mind, namely, Ed's arraignment scheduled for the next day. Lynes related the events surrounding his meeting with Monique, leaving out her father's animosity toward him. When he and Pierre retired that night, Pierre pondered Ed's arraignment, his responsibility to the village on the Little Red River, and the plans for his family and the homestead. The only thoughts that Lynes had were of the lovely Monique.

The following morning, Lynes kept himself busy preparing the wagon for the trip back to the homestead. Pierre was waiting at the office of Adams and McKay when William Brown, the law clerk, showed up to open the doors. William had his finger on everything that occurred at the law firm and knew Pierre's friend would be arraigned at 1:30 PM. Once again, William assured Pierre that McKay would be at the arraignment. William had been given the task of preparing for Ed's defense and was extremely competent and able to build a good case for the client. Whether McKay would present the defense in Ed's interest was another question.

The courthouse and the jail were in the same building, just down the street from the Prince Albert Hotel. Pierre headed for the imposing brick building to talk to Ed. It wasn't going to be easy telling Ed about his conversation with Alex the bartender.

For the second time, the young jailer led Pierre down the dark, dank cellblock to visit Ed DeGrace. It did not surprise Pierre to have Ed greet him with a big smile and quip to lighten up his unpleasant state of affairs.

"It's good to see you, Pierre. Did you bring a file?"

"I didn't have time to bake a cake, but I'll think of something."

Pierre went on to tell Ed that his arraignment was at 1:30 PM and about his attempts to see McKay. The two friends discussed the information that Alex, the bartender, related and agreed that Pierre might start scouting out a different defense attorney.

Lynes and Pierre were anxiously waiting outside the courtroom for Ed's arraignment. At one o'clock when the doors opened, they found themselves in an empty courtroom. The dark oak judge's bench sitting high above the oak witness box and stark church-like pews lent an ominous appearance to the cold, impersonal surroundings. The emptiness and dead silence gave the impression that speaking in anything other than a whisper was forbidden.

That silence was broken when the double doors opened and a well-dressed spectacled man in his forties marched in and made himself comfortable at a table in front of the bench. Alphonse Turgeon had just become the Crown's prosecutor and would later become known as one of the great statesmen in the history of Canada. Fortunately for Ed, Turgeon was a champion for civil rights and was not prejudiced against the French Metis or the Catholics' and French struggle for equal rights.

When McKay entered the courtroom, Lynes recognized the barrister as Monique's father. McKay paused where Lynes and Pierre were sitting, "This won't take long."

Before Pierre could respond, McKay whirled and walked to the front of the courtroom and shook hands with Turgeon. Pierre interpreted McKay's air of confidence as an indication that Ed was soon to be a free man. Pierre nudged Lynes and gave him a wink and a smile. Finally, the court clerk, William Horton, and the judge, James Prendergast, entered from a door behind the bench.

Pendergast was on the team of lawyers that had defended Louis Riel in that infamous trial. The jury called for that trial was all Englishmen and Scotsmen who could not speak French and were known to be hostile to the French Catholics who were demanding equal rights. Not one of the jury was challenged as the trial progressed. Only one motion was made questioning the court's legal jurisdiction, and that was denied. The defense called witnesses who were not sympathetic to Riel and as a consequence, the defense was not able to convince the judge and jury that Riel was innocent by reason of insanity. The whole defense had been presented in just one day. It took the jury only six hours to return a verdict of guilty, but mercy was recommended. Riel was sentenced to hang by Judge Hugh Richardson, in spite of the jury's request for mercy. The Prime Minister, Sir John A. McDonald is quoted as saying, "Riel will hang though every dog in Quebec shall bark."

Once again, Lynes was surprised to see another of Monique's father's companions. The young boy began to wonder about the relationship among the judge, McKay, and Treadeaux.

William Horton rose and read the charges against Ed DeGrace, "Treason against the government of Canada...that he did use force and violence for the purpose of overthrowing the government of the territory of Saskatchewan."

Prendergast looked down from the bench to James McKay. "How does your client plead?"

"Guilty, your Excellency."

Lynes and Pierre looked at each other in disbelief.

Prendergast replied, "Request for bail will be denied. Trial date is set within thirty days of today's date. Defendant will be notified." With that edict, the judge jumped up from the bench as if he had been sitting on a hot stove and almost ran from the courtroom.

McKay and Turgeon, on the other hand, rose slowly from their seats and began talking as if they had just met at an afternoon social. Lynes and Pierre sat in dumb silence as they watched the two attorneys chuckle and nod their heads in agreement. When the two finished their platitudes, McKay walked back to the two stunned observers.

"See, that didn't take long." McKay started to walk away and out of the courtroom, but Pierre jumped in front of him. Lynes had never seen his father in such a rage.

"You son of a bitch! What the hell is going on here?"

"The Queen's justice, Pierre, the Queen's justice."

With that comment, the arrogant lawyer walked around the stunned Frenchman and left the courtroom. Not one word was spoken between father and son as they stepped into the hallway. The endless hours they had shared on the trap line had taught them to give each other time to collect their thoughts in times of stress. Pierre's worst fear had just been confirmed. He knew it was not going to be easy to tell Ed about what had occurred at the arraignment.

After leaving the courtroom, Pierre went into the Mounties' headquarters to get permission to see Ed. Sgt. Major Marshall sat at his desk.

"Can I see Ed DeGrace?"

"No. Visiting hours are from six to eight, Tuesday and Friday. Come back tomorrow. I doubt he'll be going anywhere." Sgt. Marshall let out a little snicker. It took all of Pierre's willpower to check his urge to knock the snicker off the Mounties' face. Another day in Prince Albert was bound to cause worry back at his homestead so Pierre left the office.

The first light of dawn broke through the jack pine at the Dashneaux homestead. Lynes and Pierre should have been home at least twenty-four hours ago, Margarette thought, as she stood motionless at the open cabin door. Her gaze focused in the direction where her husband and son had disappeared into the forest. She did not anticipate that they would appear in the early morning hour; it would be at half day or evening if they were to return. Margarette's eyes did not see the morning light reveal the forest green and morning mist. Her vision was of her husband and son. She willed her spirit to be with them so to quell the anxiety of their delayed return. Margarette reminisced back in time to those exciting days of her youth when she first met Pierre. In her mind's eye, she pictured the strength in Pierre's face as he entered their village, pulling the wounded Watches On The Sly on a travois. The event was indelible in her mind.

"When Pierre, Big Hand, and Ed entered the village, Big Hand called out for Kiteyihtakwan (She Is Honorable), the tribe's Spirit Doctor. The villagers gathered around the wounded brave. Conspicuously absent were Runs In Circles and Tall Tree. As Kiteyihtakwan took Watches On The Sly to his parent's wigwam, the people surrounded Big Hand, asking what had happened.

"Wait! Let the owner of this weapon tell you what happened." The warrior held Tall Tree's musket high above his head. The people became silent, and all heads turned toward Tall Tree's wigwam. There was murmuring among them as they moved in the brave's direction. It seemed like an eternity to Margarette that her village people stood in silence outside of Tall Tree's home. Finally, a voice rang out from among the waiting crowd.

"Tell us what happened, Tall Tree."

"The fur-covered moose hide that covered his entrance flew aside as Tall Tree defiantly burst out of his wigwam and advanced threateningly toward Pierre. Instinctively, Pierre set himself to repel an assault. Big Hand, stopping Tall Tree's advance, threw himself at the rash brave, knocking him to the ground. When the boy jumped to his feet, he found himself face-to-face with Big Hand. The warrior was in anguish as he explored the eyes of the young man whom he had loved as if he were his own son. Big Hand had seen the look of fear and confusion in the boy's eyes many times. As a child, the brave had always sought his mentor's counsel. Appearing to ignore his mentor now, Tall Tree shouted out, "I had a vision! This white man will bring sorrow and destruction to our people. He has already taken part of our land, and he wants our women, too. I sent Watches On The Sly and Runs In Circles to save our people from this evil white man!"

"When Tall Tree ceased speaking, the moose hide moved aside as Runs In Circles stepped out of the wigwam and stood arrogantly beside Tall Tree. Margarette remembered how she was struck with fear at the words of Tall Tree and the murmuring of the people. Big Hand quickly turned and quieted his people. The villagers respected the prestige of the warrior and his prowess as a hunter and spiritual leader so they listened attentively. Big Hand knew that most of his village held Tall Tree in high regard and might believe that the brave had a vision.

His voice rang out with great authority, "Tall Tree's vision was a trick of Wisahkecahk. If his vision was true, he would not have sent someone else to do away with this man. A warrior does not send someone else to slay his enemies."

"Big Hand did not get to continue with his thoughts of calling for a counsel meeting of the elders to decide what should be done for as he spoke, Tall Tree drew his knife and lunged at Pierre. The blade sliced across Pierre's back as he threw himself at Tall Tree's legs, knocking the brave face down on the ground. Pierre was on his feet in an instant, skinning knife in hand. Crouched like a cougar ready to spring, Pierre yielded the flashing blade in circles at the end of his outstretched arm.

"Come and get it, you son of a bitch!"

"Tall Tree advanced slowly toward Pierre. Big Hand could sense the lack of confidence and bravado the young brave was trying to conceal. This was the first time in his life that he faced the possibility of death. His teacher and mentor was not going to allow that catastrophe to happen. Once again, Big Hand placed himself between the two adversaries.

"There will be no killing here today!"

"Big Hand still had Tall Tree's musket in his hands, and he threw it angrily at Tall Tree. The brave dropped his knife as he tried to catch the musket. The gun flew through the air with such force that it knocked Tall Tree back and fell to the ground. Before the brave could reach down and pick up his rifle, he found himself face-to-face with Big Hand. As a father feels when he looks into the face of his desperate child, Big Hand observed the look of desperation and fear in Tall Tree's eyes.

"This will be settled without blood. Isn't it enough that Watches On The Sly may be dying? Has not the Great Spirit told us that all life is sacred? We will ask Mistapew if he will tell us what brought this trouble to our village. Mistapew is the spirit of the Shaking Tent. He can give information on events (past and present or future), on why someone is sick or acts the way he or she does. The spirit can also locate valuable lost items and aid in deciding where to hunt. The ritual must be observed at night because Maskote Pisike (The Buffalo) and Miskinaw (The Turtle) are the Shaking Tent's spirits. The buffalo is the constellation Perseus, and the turtle is Capella, the brightest star in the constellation of Aurigae the Charioteer."

"As it is with most cultures, the First Nations' peoples looked to the heavens for guidance. The ritual begins when a strong spiritual member of the tribe builds a tent. He is then bound and hidden in a wigwam. He begins by singing and beating on drums to call on Maskote Pisike, Mikinaw, and Mistapew. If he has special powers, Ochek Atchakosuk,

The Fisher (The Big Dipper) will join in to help the other spirits. The tent begins to shake when the spirits respond, and they untie the one who called them. That person exits the wigwam and then speaks with Mistapew, and the spirits speak in turn through him to those who are present.

"As Big hand spoke, Margarette pictured in her mind running to Pierre and throwing her arms around him in a protective embrace. She recalled the shock of seeing blood on her hands when he gently pushed her away. Pierre stood, knife in hand with Ed by his side as the people gathered around Big Hand and Tall Tree. The skinning knife slowly slid back into its sheath when the people moved toward the center of the village to hold council. Margarette grabbed Pierre by the arm, urgently pulling him toward her wigwam. He wasn't aware that he had been cut until he saw the blood on Margarette's hands. It was then that he felt a stinging sensation just below his shoulders and the wetness on his back. A leather container of salve made from the bark of the juniper hung from one of the wigwam poles. Tenderly, Margarette applied the salve to Pierre's wound. She remembered as she treated the wound how she leaned over and kissed him lovingly on his shoulder.

"You will stay here tonight. I will take care of you."

"Margarette removed Pierre's moccasins and trousers and washed the blood from his body. She then covered him with a soft rabbit fur blanket and lay down beside him, caressing his shoulders, neck, and hair until he drifted off to blissful sleep. As the maid lay snuggled close to Pierre, the sound of the Shaking Tent drums echoed through the village.

There was little doubt that Big Hand was the highest spiritual leader of the village. He accepted the request of the elders that he perform the Shaking Tent ceremony. Eager to defuse the conflict, he and Walks On Water hastily constructed a canvas-covered dome tent at the edge of the village clearing. Kicikawi-Pisim (The Sun) disappeared in the west, and the fires surrounding the Shaking Tent cast eerie shadows of the wigwams as the two danced into the night. Near the tent, two bear skulls hung from fresh cut poles. The poles were hung in reverence and respect to the most intelligent and powerful spirit of all land animals. The animals would return and give themselves to the

Cree people. Both poles were decorated with paint and colorful ribbons fluttering in the night air. The flickering of the firelight upon the skulls made them appear to nod in approval of the ritual they were witnessing. The people sat huddled around the fires in whispered conversations as all eyes stayed affixed on the Shaking Tent.

"The monotonous drumming and chanting went on well into the night as an early spring chill fell over the village. Soon there was silence and heads began to nod. Only the sounds from Big Hand and the crackling of the fires captured the night.

"Just before dawn when all the stars were visible in the eastern sky, the villagers became alert to the sounds of the horses stomping nervously in their corral, and then the village dogs began to howl and bark as in distress. The howl of the timber wolf and the screams of the cougar violated the morning quietness. From the west, a warm, gentle breeze caused the ribbons hanging from the bear skulls to flap in the wind., the drums continued to beat. The Chinook wind grew warmer and stronger as it began to howl through the Jack pine that surrounded the village. The people trembled when a powerful gust swept through the village, creating a whirlwind that danced around the canvas tent. The tent shook like a dog coming out of the water, then, instantly, the drumming stopped and the Chinook fled. The early spring chill of the night once again settled on the village as Big Hand emerged from among the wigwams. He was wrapped in his ceremonial garb of bear and wolf. Walking slowly as if in a trance, he stopped in front of his people. A chill ran through the listeners when the warrior spoke in a voice sounding like the angry growl of Misipisiw (The Cougar Spirit).

"The vision of Tall Tree was given to him by Wisakechahk (The Trickster). Tall Tree did not seek the understanding of an elder. The Vision was a warning that his jealousy of Pierre would bring shame to his people. Tall Tree and Runs In Circles will leave our village. They will seek another tribe. After many Vision Quests, they will regain their honor. Walks On The Sly will live. He will stay with his people as a reminder of the evil of jealousy. He will be given a new name."

"Margarette remembered that day as if it were yesterday, how when her father returned to the wigwam, he tenderly touched her head as she lay snuggled close to Pierre, and quietly chuckled.

"My daughter is baiting her trap."

"Recalling the cherished times she had with Pierre and Lynes was the only way that Margarette could relieve herself of the worry she had for their safe return. Oliver was watching his mother from within the cabin. Her vision was interrupted when she felt her oldest son's hand on her shoulder.

"Don't worry wimaw (Wimaw was short for Okawimaw (Mother). Dad and Lynes can take care of themselves. They are probably just having a good time in Prince Albert."

Margarette's eyebrows raised as she looked sideways at Oliver, "They better not be!"

When the pair left the courthouse, Lynes wanted to tell Pierre that he had seen McKay and the Judge with Monique's father the night before the trial, but he could see that Pierre was trying to overcome his anger. It was no time for idle conversation. Lynes knew the two of them were long overdue on their return to the homestead. He also felt that leaving Ed in jail without doing everything that they could to see that he would be treated fairly was their moral obligation. The year, 1907, was not a good time to be a French Metis in Saskatchewan. In previous years, the Metis had been an independent and proud majority in what was then called "Rupert's Land." Ruper was the King's cousin and the head of the Hudson Bay Company. Along with the other Indians, the French-Metis were a valuable and needed human resource for two major fur companies: the Hudson Bay Company and the Northwest Company. By royal proclamation, the Hudson Bay Company ruled Rupert's Land.

The early French trappers were romantically called "Voyagers". For 200 years, through mixed marriages with the First Nations' people, they developed their own culture and identity. Their language was a mixture of Indian and French. Distinguished by their long-hooded blue coat (Capote) and a colorful beaded "Possible Bag" hanging from a multi-colored sash, they were recognized as a distinct and separate people. The Hudson Bay Company granted them 116,000 square miles in the Red River Valley, and they developed villages and outposts all along the fur trade routes from then on. Such trade routes were measured in "Pipes". About every five or six miles, the Metis would pull a pipe out of their

Possible Bag and take a smoke break. The Metis were also instrumental in establishing the border between Canada and America.

In 1870, Canada bought the Hudson Bay Company and began to settle the Northwest Territories. To make room for the settlers (labor force), to exploit the natural resources and support commercial interests, it was necessary to repress and disperse those who inhabited the land. The first treaty by the Crown was signed in 1871. By 1906, eight more treaties were forced upon the aboriginal people; the Crown recognized the Metis as aboriginal. In the past, there had been a political, educational, and legal system that was designed to do away with their society. Unlike the Frist Nations' peoples who were recognized as a people, the French-Metis were now denigrated by the press and political propaganda as Half-breeds and rebels (terrorists). Using the Northwest Rebellion, Prime Minister John A. McDonald, unscrupulous politicians, con men, and speculators were successful in reducing the French-Metis to second-class citizens. When a new prime minister who had sympathy for the Metis came on the scene, he is known to have said, "Our prisons are full of men who, despairing ever to get justice by peace, sought to obtain by war, who despairing of being treated like freemen, took their lives in their own hands rather than be treated as slaves." Those were the words of Wilfred Laurier, but the damage had been done.

It was clear to Lynes that they would have to seek out someone who was not prejudiced against "Half-breeds". He had never known prejudice from his father or his mother's people but was becoming acutely aware of the distinctions among classes in society. For the first time in his life, he began to become self-conscious about his dress. He proudly touched his sash.

At last Pierre spoke. It was a rhetorical question that Lynes had heard many times. "Well, son, what do we do now?"

Pierre knew what the answer would be. "Get a different attorney."

There were only four other law firms in town that were not owned by McKay or the judge. All were willing to take the case, but only one was able to dispel Pierre's suspicions. Algernon Doak was not fond of James McKay. His only assurance to Pierre was that he would keep Ed from the rope. It seemed clear to Lynes, however, that there was little hope for Ed DeGrace. He came close to tears for fear that tomorrow might be the last time he would get to see his dear friend.

Lynes glanced up at the big wall clock in the law office of Algernon Doak, His preoccupation with getting help for Ed caused him to forget that he had a five o'clock rendezvous with Monique at the Presbyterian church. Lynes's anxiety was lifted as he envisioned his enticing enchantress passionately waiting to see him again. He was struck with the conflict of whether to stay with his father for moral support or to meet with the golden haired beauty. His testosterone level made the decision for him.

"Dad, I think Monique may be waiting for me at the church. Do you need me for anything in the next hour or so?"

Pierre jokingly replied, "Go ahead, son. While you're there, you might take time to say a prayer for Ed and our family."

As Lynes hurried to the church, he glimpsed himself in the reflection of the storefront windows. Seeing his image that way made him feel somehow different about himself. He began to lose the confidence he had in himself when he had first crossed the North Saskatchewan on the ferry. His extended stay in Prince Albert had made him sharply aware of the class distinctions and prejudices that plagued society. He wondered if Monique's father would accept him if he wore fancy clothes rather than his customary clothing.

Lynes felt beads of sweat in his armpits as he slowly opened the cathedral door. He felt his heart beat faster when he saw Monique sitting in the pew where they first met. It was past the hour, and he was relieved to see her there. Beams of light shone through the stained glass windows, highlighting the blue ribbon in Monique's golden locks. She acted as if she were unaware of his presence when Lynes sat down beside her. Her silence indicated to Lynes that she was in prayer. When he bowed his head to pray, she spoke.

"I thought you weren't going to come today."

"I am glad that I did, and I am happy that you are here."

Monique turned to Lynes and laid her hand on his arm. "And I am happy that you are here! There is so much I would like to know about you and this wild country. You are so handsome. You must live an exciting life."

Lynes vividly recalled the last words he had heard from Monique's father.

"It's going to get a lot more exciting if your father finds out I came here to meet you. He told me to stay away from you."

There was both guilt and fear in his voice. Guilt because he had disobeyed an elder's orders and fear that he might never be with his love again. He had learned at an early age from his father and his mother's people that the orders of elders were to be respected. Orders given by an elder in Lynes's culture were only to protect someone from harm. He felt it was his obligation to tell Monique of her father's command.

Monique kew she was forbidden to see Lynes, but her hunger for independence and excitement prompted her to disobey. After turning thirteen, she had become increasingly belligerent. It was at her governess's suggestion that Robert Treadeaux take his daughter on a vacation to the frontier. The rationale was that being in unfamiliar surroundings would increase the girl's dependency upon her father. However, the real motive for the suggestion was the desire of the governess to take a break from the unruly young woman.

"Don't worry. He still thinks I'm a little girl. I'm old enough to make my own decisions."

Monique's tone of voice rose in anger, "If I want to see you, he can't stop me. He is always trying to select my friends and ordering me what to do. Sometimes he makes me so angry!"

Lynes was taken aback by Monique's defiance and the anger in her voice. None of the young women he knew in his mother's village expressed such disobedience to their fathers. He was torn between his desire to hold her in his arms and to be consumed by her love, and his instinct to avoid danger. Caution was thrown to the wind, when once again she spoke in a soft and tender voice that melted his heart.

"Tell me, Bien-aime (beloved), will you be in the city long? I want to spend more time with you." With that, Monique leaned over and gave Lynes a tender kiss on his cheek.

Her question plunged Lynes back into the turmoil that had surrounded him since Ed had been arrested, but the gentle kiss heightened his desires. He fought to overcome his impulse to reach out and pull Monique to him and feel the warmth of her supple body against his own, to taste the sweetness of her lips.

Pierre had decided that he would take the supplies up North. Lynes would stay in Prince Albert and work with Algernon Doak until Ed's fate was decided. Lynes was to keep Ed supplied with whatever he needed to make his jail stay more comfortable. Since he would be in town anyway, Lynes would work at the sawmill.

Days later Lynes said to Monique, "I will be here as long as I can help my friend. I don't know how long that will be."

"What kind of help does your friend need?"

Lynes choked as he answered her question. It was a relief for him to avert his attention from her comeliness to explain the events that had occurred in the last few days. To reveal his feelings and share his troubles was out of character for Lynes, but he opened up like a floodgate when he began to talk. He felt like a burden was lifted from him as he shared his problems and emotions with Monique. She found it extremely interesting that Ed's lawyer and the judge were associates of her father. Both men had lavished her with their attention from the moment they had met. James McKay seemed to be particularly close to her father, and she considered him to be a good friend.

"Mister McKay has been so kind to me. If I can find a way to talk to him, maybe he will try to help your friend."

For an instant, Monique's words gave Lynes a glimmer of hope, but just as quickly he thought it was unlikely that McKay would change his attitude. He never told Monique the part where his father had called McKay a son of a bitch.

"Thank you for wanting to help, but my father has found another lawyer for Ed. I didn't mean to burden you with my problems. Please forgive me."

As Lynes spoke, he still felt the warmth of Monique's tender kiss. Other than his mother, this was his first kiss. He was confused and embarrassed by his extreme physical and emotional reaction to it. Although he was curious about sex, none of the girls in the village aroused his interest so he rejected their advances. He was just about to ask Monique if he could kiss her when the Reverend Colin Young made himself known to the would-be lovers. He had been working on the Sunday sermon near the pulpit and couldn't help but overhear the couple's conversation.

Colin was in his late twenties, but the premature graying of his temples hid his youth. He was slightly overweight, which made him look shorter than he already was. There was a twinkle in his eyes, and he had a sense of humor that was more characteristic of a vaudeville comic than a minister. When appropriate, he was capable of transforming his demeanor to that of a sage. His appearance at the pulpit surprised Lynes and Monique.

"Brothers and sisters, we are gathered here today..." Feigning surprise at the couple's presence, the Reverend looked down at the startled pair, his head cocked to one side, and a quizzical expression on his smiling round face.

"Why are we here today?"

Colin jumped down from the pulpit with the agility of an athlete, laughing all the time. His laughter could only be described as the cackling of a chicken with a bad cold. In spite of that fact, Colin's laughter was contagious so Lynes and Monique couldn't hold back their smiles.

"Hello, Monique, I see you've brought me a convert."

With a quiet laugh, Monique introduced Lynes. Colin reached out and gave Lynes a firm handshake. "I envy you my good fellow; I am only graced with Monique's presence on Sunday." He ended with a high-pitched giggle.

A bit perturbed by Colin's interruption, all Lynes could come up with was a quiet, "Hello."

It was choir practice night at St. Paul's Church, and Colin was expecting the singers to start showing up at any moment. "I have a noisy crowd showing up at any time now. If you want to hear yourself think, a walk in the park out back would be better suited. Lynes, it is nice meeting you."

And then in a more serious tone of voice, Colin stated, "If you have the time in a couple of hours after the choir leaves, I would like to talk with you."

When Lynes and Monique left the church, Lynes was wondering what Colin wanted to talk to him about. He could only assume that it was going to be about his relationship with Monique.

Daylight hours in Northern Saskatchewan began to lengthen in the early spring, but they were much too short for Lynes. Red, gold, and yellow shone in the western sky as Lynes walked Monique back to the church where their rendezvous would end. As the young people neared the church, the choir's song became familiar, "Just A Closer Walk With Thee."

Later, as Lynes watched Monique disappear into the hotel, he was left with the joy of having been with her, yet exasperated by the briefness of their meeting. He started to walk back to the church but changed his mind. After meeting up with his father, Lynes no longer felt the urgent need for a talk with Reverend Young.

The following day was spent waiting to see Ed and getting everything ready for Pierre's trip back to the homestead. Pierre gave Lynes, Ed's share of the fur sale with instructions to be cautious and frugal. To save money, Lynes planned on moving out of the hotel and setting up camp on the outskirts of Prince Albert. Interesting as it was, Lynes felt uncomfortable in the city.

The two headed back to Sgt. Marshall's office. Lynes, filled with anxiety, feared that he might not get to see Ed. In addition, that fear was compounded by his concern that Pierre's seething anger toward the Mountie would result in a physical confrontation. He imagined Ed in chains, a beaten and demoralized man. Once again, Sgt. Major Marshall, amusing himself, smirked at Pierre.

"What can I do for you?"

Lynes could see his father was about to explode. He grabbed him by the arm and addressed the Mountie. "We've come to get your permission to see Ed DeGrace."

Marshall picked up his telephone and connected with the jail turnkey. "Hey! Peter, is Ed DeGrace receiving guests tonight?" The Mountie snickered.

Forsyth responded, "One at a time."

Lynes sat down on a long bench near Marshall's desk to wait his turn to visit with Ed. Marshall watched Lynes as he looked around the office, obviously avoiding looking in the officer's direction.

In his many years as a Mountie, Marshall had become an expert at reading the faces of those with whom he came in contact. As he observed Lynes, he saw an expression that was etched on his mind. Lynes's expression was that of his own son's at critical moments in his life, a son the Mountie had not seen in years. He saw the anxiety and confusion that are the encumbrances of the innocence of youth. Marshall felt an urge to connect with the young man.

"Hey, young fella, want a cuppa coffee or something?"

"No, thank you." Lynes wasn't aware that Mounties were addressed as "Sir".

"Is that your dad that you came in with?"

"Yes."

Marshall was considering how he wanted his own relationship with his son to be when he stated, "Looks to me like you and your dad get along pretty good."

Lynes nodded his head in the affirmative and before Marshall could speak again, Lynes got up and walked over to the door that Pierre had exited. He looked back at Marshall sitting at his desk. As their eyes met, Lynes discerned a lurking sadness in the Mountie's eyes.

As Lynes entered the cellblock with Forsyth, he wondered how anyone could work in such a place of utter hopelessness. His misgivings were dispelled when he saw Ed, elbow resting on the bars, a smile on his face, taking long satisfying puffs on his pipe. His voice was as jovial as if he had just heard a good joke.

"Damned if it ain't good to see your smiling face. Gotta thank you for the tobacco and grub you and your dad brought. I'm doin' just fine now."

In truth, Ed had not been "doin' just fine" in the last thirteen hours before Lynes's visit. It was common practice in 1907 for unscrupulous prison wardens to hire prisoners out to equally unscrupulous businesses. The rationale was to support the prisons, but more often than not, the practice was used to line the pockets of the wardens. Ed's day started out at 5:00 AM with an hour and a half wagon ride to the coal mines, followed by ten hours underground, chipping out coal, and then the ride back to Prince Albert. He was accompanied on his trips by a tall, dignified Indian, Acahkos-Okohp (Star Blanket) and a short, fat Indian, Mistahcikew (Eats A Lot). Both were serving time for opposing a logging operation on what they considered their land.

Lynes was shocked by Ed's appearance. He was covered from head to toe with black dust. His face, enveloped in black dust, showed lines of sweat that revealed the true color of his skin. Lynes felt as if he were in the middle of a nightmare. Anguish gripped him as he stood helpless, unable to rescue a loved one from the hands of destruction. It took every fiber in his body to fight back the urge to cry outwardly, Kisemanito (God), save my friend! Struggling to hide the pain he felt, Lynes smiled back at Ed.

"It's good to see you, too, Ed. I didn't recognize you for a minute there." The smile left his young face. "What the heck have they got you doing?"

Every bone in Ed's body ached, and it was an effort just to stand at the cell door. Even the smile he displayed to ease the worry he saw on Lynes's face was exhausting. Pierre had told Ed how troubled Lynes was over his arrest.

"Ain't nothin' I can't handle, son. Don't you worry. As long as I got my smokes and good friends like you and your dad, ain't nothin' they can throw at me I can't handle."

"I'll make sure you don't run out of tobacco. You can count on that."

Ed continued his charade. "I know I can. I had a good talk with your dad, and he filled me in on what's happening. I guess he told you that I'm counting on you to take care of Spade and my Henry."

"I sure will."

Ed reached through the bars, his hand beckoning for Lynes to come closer. Lynes felt the strength of Ed's calloused hand on the back of his neck. He saw the twinkle in Ed's eyes that he had seen on many occasions when he was about to tell a joke.

"OK, then. Now you get your ass out of this hell hole and go take care of yourself."

Lynes was disappointed that Ed was ending their visit.

"I'll be back. Is there anything you want me to bring you?"

Ed forced a wide smile. "I'll make a list. Now get the hell out of here!"

As Lynes was led out of the cellblock, he felt a bond between Ed and him like he had never felt before. His mind raced on, thinking about what he could do to make life easier for his friend. After signing up for his next visit with Ed at the Mounties' headquarters, Lynes was stopped as he was about to leave.

"Hold up there; I want to talk with you for a minute."

Marshall spoke in a stern voice; he had already suspected that the warden was up to no good. His suspicions were heightened previously when Pierre left his office and without looking at him said, "That's one hell of a way to treat a human being!"

Marshall wanted to get to know the young man. "What's your name?"

Lynes hesitated, wondering why the Mountie wanted to know his name. "Lynes Dashneaux."

"Your father was pretty hot when he left here. I don't want him to get into trouble." Marshall was hoping his concern for Lynes's father would open a line of communication between Lynes and him.

"He won't." Lynes was in no mood for conversation.

"OK, then. Tell him I'm going to look in on your friend." There was a tone of reassurance in Marshall's voice that gave Lynes a better feeling about the Mountie as he left the office.

The icy cold water of the Northern Saskatchewan River slapped at the sides of the ferry as it carried Lynes and Pierre back from whence they came. It was approaching nightfall, and they were going to camp on the road back to the homestead for the night. Pierre wanted to get an early start on his trip north. That evening there were long stretches of silence between the father and son, occasionally broken by warnings from Pierre on what to watch out for in an environment with which the son was not that familiar. Lynes had heard it all before on the trip down to Prince Albert, but he still listened patiently. Lynes's thoughts were on the lovely Monique and when they would meet again.

On his trip north, Pierre met with Wild Goose and Andrea Beauchene. Those two were on their way to find out why Lynes and Pierre had not returned to their homestead. Wild Goose continued with Pierre, and Beauchene headed for Prince Albert to inform Lynes of a Metis colony south of town where friends of Beauchene would accept him. Pierre was relieved to know that Lynes would be in the company of people who were familiar with the Prince Albert culture.

Beauchene was a formidable figure. The bushy hair and extensive beard gave his head the appearance that it was oversized for an unusually large body. The man's 272 pounds was hidden in a six-foot-three inch frame that carried very little fat. Without exerting himself, Beauchene could hike stride for stride with a horse and for a longer period of time. Not a slave to fashion, his buckskins were rough and stained with sweat and whatever else with which he came in contact. As much a part of him as his right hand was the large dog that never left his side. Wolf was a pup from Thunder, the dog that was a gift from Big Hand to Pierre. Fortunately for those with whom the pair came in contact, both Wolf and Beauchene were mild mannered and slow to anger.

With Monique always in the back of his mind, Lynes was laying out his plans for the future without his father or mother being near at hand. As he crossed back over the Northern Saskatchewan River, he felt entirely alone, surrounded by uncertainty and the unknown. It gave him a strange feeling of excitement and energy. He was excited that he was about to embark upon a new way of life and and charged with the energy and optimism of youth. When Ed's horse, Spade, trotted off the ferry, Lynes sat straight up and bowed his head before he entered busy River Street. He prayed to Kise-Manito (God) thanking him for his good fortune and for guidance to walk a safe path.

Lynes tied Spade in front of Algernon Doak's office. It was too early for the lawyer's door to open so Lynes just stood by the building and entertained himself by watching the people and traffic on River Street. Several men stopped and slowed down to admire the handsome Morgan horse, adorned with a colorful beaded moose bone saddle sporting a Henry rifle in a fringed scabbard. Lynes became concerned when a Mountie came by and stopped in front of Spade. After walking around the horse, obviously looking for a Hudson Bay or Cavalry brand, he turned to Lynes.

"Is this your horse and rifle?"

Lynes anticipated the question but was unsure what his answer should be. His hesitation gave the Mountie reason to question his response. "I'm taking care of them for a friend."

"Where's your friend?"

Once again, Lynes hesitated. "He's in jail, waiting for his trial."

Lynes got a sick feeling in his stomach as the Mountie untied Spade and motioned with his head for Lynes to follow.

"You better come with me."

Tranquility turned to chaos for Lynes as he walked in front of the Mountie in the direction of the Northwest Mounted Police headquarters. Filled with anxiety, Lynes dreaded the thought that he would have to tell Ed that Spade had been taken from him.

The Mountie took the Henry from the scabbard and motioned with it for Lynes to go into the headquarters' office. Once inside, the Mountie grabbed Lynes by the arm.

"Sgt. Major, I've got a young fellow who claims he's taking care of this rifle and a horse outside. He says they belong to one of our prisoners." The Mountie seated Lynes down at Marshall's desk.

Marshall was both surprised and pleased to see Lynes again. Ironically, he had just addressed a letter to his son, a letter he had written the day before after he had talked to Lynes. Shortly after Lynes had left Marshall's office, the Mountie walked over to the courthouse to check on Ed DeGrace. Ed was passed out on his bunk; his food tray sat on the floor, untouched.

Seeing Ed's condition, Marshall was curious as to how many more prisoners the warden had working in the coal mines. Unable to find the culprit, Marshall informed Peter Forsyth that Ed and the two Indians were not to leave the courthouse until he had a talk with the warden. With the previous evening's visit to the jail on his mind, the Mountie gave Lynes a reassuring smile.

"Hello, Lynes. I didn't expect you back until Friday. Where's your dad?"

The genuine concern in Marshall's voice did little to dispel the turmoil and confusion that engulfed Lynes. Pierre and Ed had warned him that the "Men in Red Coats" had power over everyone, and it was unsafe to question their authority. Lynes had no fear of the Mountie but recalled the warnings.

"He went back home."

"Where's home?"

"About twelve smokes north." (60 miles)

"How long do you figure you'll be in town?" Marshall could see that the young trapper was out of his element.

"Until I find out what you are going to do with my friend."

"Hold on a minute."

Marshall picked up his telephone and asked to be connected to the jail. "This is Sgt. Major Marshall. I want to talk to one of your prisoners, Ed DeGrace. I EXPECT him to be there." The last statement referred to his orders from the night before.

At least five minutes of silence passed as Lynes sat staring at the telephone, wondering if the strange contraption was going to work. Finally, Marshall spoke, "I've got a young man here who says he's taking care of your horse and rifle."

The long silence that followed gave Lynes cause to wonder again if and how the telephone worked. At last, Marshall hung up the earpiece. "OK. OK."

While the Mountie was talking to Ed and as he listened to Ed's response, he stared intensely into Lynes's eyes. Once again, he saw the eyes of his son. He did have the authority to confiscate the sorely needed horse and rifle. Good mounts were in short supply in Northern Saskatchewan, and the Henry would look good hanging from the saddle of a Mountie. Marshall saw his chance to gain the young trapper's confidence.

"Well, Lynes, Ed said you were taking care of his horse and rifle all right, but since they're his, they can be confiscated. I'm going to let you take care of the horse, but as long as you're in town, we'll hold on to the rifle. You're going to be in Prince Albert for a while if you're waiting for your friend's trial. If you feel like you have a need to talk to somebody, you can come on by."

After Lynes left, Marshall turned to the Corporal who had brought Lynes in, "Keep an eye on that kid; he's green as a cucumber. I don't want him gittin' in trouble...eh."

After Lynes left the Mountie headquarters building, his mind was awhirl with what had just transpired. It took a while for him to get his mind refocused on how he had planned to stay in Prince Albert. After mulling over his situation, Lynes found himself back on River Street at the office of Algernon Doak. After asking Algernon all the questions he could to reassure himself that Ed was not going to be hung, Lynes continued on with his plans. It was not by accident that on his way to the Prince Albert Lumber Company, Lynes rode by the Prince Albert Hotel, his eyes constantly on the lookout for the golden-haired Monique.

Going to work for the Prince Albert Lumber Company was the first step in Lynes's plan. The company belonged to a group of East Coast American lumber barons. By 1907, most of the Eastern United States had been deforested. The vast boreal forests of North Saskatchewan were ripe for the picking.

Employing around 2,000 people, the Prince Albert Lumber Company was the largest employer in Prince Albert. The vigorous campaign waged by the government to populate the new territory resulted in an over abundant work force. A long line of men could be found every morning at the mill's hiring office. That line was made up of homesteaders, immigrants, loggers, and other workers who came out West seeking a new life. The government and investors with interests in the land and natural resources of Northern Saskatchewan had rallied a huge work force. The population in Prince Albert increased from around 1700 to over 6,000 from 1900 to 1910. There were almost 50,000 people in Saskatchewan alone when just a few years before there had only been 14,000. Lynes watched as man after man was turned away from the hiring window. He was confident that he wouldn't be turned away. Mr. Mattis, the superintendent, had promised him a job whenever he wanted to go to work. Lynes waited in line for almost an hour before he reached the window.

"What's your name?"

The dispatcher scribbled Lynes's name on a card. "What kind of experience do you have?"

Lynes told him that he was a trapper. On the next line, the dispatcher wrote, <u>Hunter, interpreter, Metis.</u>

The man looked up at Lynes, "We got nothing today. Next."

Lynes thought there was some kind of mistake. "Mister Mattis said I could get a job here."

"I don't know no Mattis; now move along." The next man in line stepped in front of Lynes.

Undeterred, Lynes rode over to the mill office but Mattis was home with his sick daughter. The next thing on Lynes's list was finding a good campsite on the outskirts of Prince Albert. He would camp there until he got a job at the mill.

The Company supplied board and room for their employees. In fact, they built one-bedroom houses for families and a boarding house for single men. At the end of the month the board and room would be deducted from the worker's pay, along with anthing else they acquired at the company store. The balance of their pay was given to them in Script, money that was printed by the company and only good at the company store. Wages were well calculated so that if an employee purchased anything above the bare necessities, he would receive little or no pay. Seventeen cents an hour didn't leave much room for extravagance, not when a pair of boots cost $3.00. Lynes was unaware of the unprincipled practices of the lumber barons at that point. While he was searching for a campsite, he was thinking of how he would be able to make life easier for his family with the fortune he was going to make working at the sawmill.

Determined to be first in line at the mill, Lynes rose early the next morning. Splashing himself in the ice-cold water of the North Saskatchewan River, he got the jolt he needed to wake up. Chewing on a chunk of pemmican, Lynes gave Spade a quick rub down and a sugar cube. When Spade heard Lynes's whistle, he expected and received a sugar cube. In the darkness, Lynes gave Spade his head as they made their way toward Prince Albert. Arriving two hours befoe the hiring office window opened, Lynes was surprised to see a dozen men already standing in line. Lynes took his place in line.

Within minutes the line bagan to form behind him. After a while, the man behind him got his attention. "How long you been here?"

"Not long." Lynes recognized the man's accent as Metis.

"Ain't been much hiring lately. Somebody got to quit, get fired, or die before they put anybody on."

The stranger seemed eager to tell Lynes how desperate he was to get a job. As Lynes listened to the story of a wife and two hungry children, he had the impulse to give the stranger his place in line. After stepping in front of Lynes, the stranger tried to strike up a conversation with the man in front of him. When he was ignored, he turned back to Lynes.

"Have you tried to get in on the bridge job? They're starting to build a bridge to get a train across the river. Could be they'll be needing workers."

By 1907, the ferries couldn't handle all the commercial traffic crossing the North Saskatchewan River. The Canadian Northern Railway was beginning construction on a bridge, opening Prince Albert up to both sides of the river. Sir William McKenzie and Sir Donald Mann were given generous gifts of public (Indian) land and public money to build another railway to open up the West. Not satisfied with the profits, gifts, and bond guarantees given to them from Ottawa, the shysters managed to fleece the Province of Saskatchewan out of another $60,000 to build the bridge. The Canadian government followed the U. S. model of lining the pockets of the well connected. It didn't matter much to Lynes for whom he worked. All he wanted to do was make life easier for his family. His conversation with the stranger opened up opportunities for employment that he had not thought of previously. By the time Lynes reached the hiring window, he had a list in mind of every place he would go that day to find work if he weren't hired here.

The first stop would be to see if A. L. Mattis, the general manager who promised him employment was in his office. That first step was taken when Lynes walked into Mr. Mattis' office just as the manager looked up in surprise, "Hi, how have you been?"

"Pretty good, but I would be doing better if I had a job."

The first meeting Mattis had with Lynes was still fresh in his mind. Unaware of any openings suitable for a young trapper, he had made inquiries among his foremen. Believing himself to be a man of his word with integrity, Mattis would see to it that Lynes was hired. From his perspective, he was being generous by giving Lynes a means of survival. He gave no thought that he would not have a job if it were not for the companies' exploitation of desperate men and the environment. In order to exploit the wealth of the West, the government and corporations in early Canada compromised human rights in the name of progress. Mattis had compassion for individuals with whom he came in contact, but he was caught up in the ideology of progress for profit.

"You'll have a job in the next couple of days. Just keep showing up at the hiring office. I'll see to it. Have you got a place to stay?"

"Got a campsite upriver."

Mattis scribbled a note on a piece of paper and handed it to Lynes. "Here, take this up the street to the boarding house. If they have a room, you can bunk there." The boarding house was in a complex of buildings consisting of a day room with a pool hall, equipment barns, 40 company houses and the company store.

Lynes thanked Mattis when he left the manager's office. Both he and Mattis were feeling good about themselves.

There was no room at the boarding house. Men were sleeping on the floors and packed in like sardines. Lynes preferred his campsite to the boarding house. There was plenty of daylight left for Lynes to scout out the opportunities the stranger had told him about. In additon, Lynes intended on being at the church promptly at five o'clock. Lynes's curiosity about the horseless carriages on the streets of Prince Albert prompted him to stop at the Calgary Garage Company on First Avenue. Henry Downey, the manager and salesman, was eager to show as well as expound upon the advantages of the automobile. Lynes was privileged to be able to climb up and sit behind the steering wheel of the shiny, black Pope-Toledo. The plush padded leather seats were as comfortable as the chairs in the hotel lounge. Lynes thought, 'One day I'm going to have one of these.' Lost in fantasy, he was awakened by a familiar voice.

"Are you going to buy that contraption Chiot (French for puppy)?"

"Andrea! Wolf! What are you doing here?"

Seeing Andrea and Wolf was always a treat. Beauchene made conversation a form of entertainment. He was always ready with a tall tale or witty metaphor.

"Pierre asked me to come down here to keep your balls out of the fire."

He went on to tell Lynes about the Metis colony and the advantage of getting acquainted with people who were familiar with the district. "I got a bunch of real close friends down there; throw a stick and you might hit one of my kids." Beauchene let out a hearty laugh.

Spade could feel Beauchene's heavy hand on his shoulder as they made their way to the Metis colony. Walking stride for stride with Spade, Andrea filled Lynes in on the situation at the homestead and the status of his mother and siblings. His mind at ease concerning his family, Lynes asked Andrea how his trip to Prince Albert went. Beauchene couldn't pass up the opportunity to share a recent event.

"Coming round a corner on the trail, me and Wolf came face-to-face with the biggest grizzly bear you ever saw. He wasn't 'bout to make way for me and Wolf. And me and Wolf weren't gonna make room for no bear. Wolf let out a growl and that bear let out a growl and stood up on his hind legs. Musta been ten feet tall. I took off my cap and throwed it at his face. When he took a swipe at the hat, I had my knife out and gutted him right there on the trail. Haw! Haw! Had him half skinned out before he hit the ground. Haw! Haw! It took Wolf damn near an hour to clean up the mess. The only thing Wolf didn't eat was his asshole." Lynes laughed until his stomach hurt. For a long time nothing was said, only an occasional chuckle when he thought back on Beauchene's bear tale.

Some of the dwellings in the settlement were made of logs, and others constructed of lumber from the sawmills along the North Saskatchewan River. An occasional canvas wigwam, animal shelter, and barn spotted the landscape. The buildings spread out for over a mile in each direction. Dirt roads, deeply rutted by Red River carts and freight wagons, united the community as one. Gardens of cabbage, corn, garlic, and other food produce that grew in the harsh Saskatchewan climate formed blankets of green and gold in patchwork patterns. Women in long dresses and buckskin leggings labored in the gardens. Their colorful blouses with beadwork designs caught Lynes's imagination. He pictured his mother working in the garden at the homestead. A woman weeding her garden near the road, glanced up to see the passers by and screamed out.

"Andrea!"

Andrea looked up at Lynes and in a low, mischievous voice muttered, "Uh, Oh."

"You've come back! You've come back!" The woman's voice rang with exuberance as she ran toward Andrea with her arms outstretched. She had to jump up to hug Andrea around the neck. Her moccasins were two feet off the ground. It appeared to Lynes as if she were going to become a permanent fixture hanging off Andrea until he finally broke her grip and held her at arm's length.

"Danged if you ain't still as cute as a speckled puppy."

After introducing the woman to Lynes and accepting an invitation to an evening meal, the two men arrived at the cabin of Joe Doucette. They were welcomed by an old First Nations' woman. Her hair was long and white and glistened like the snow on a clear, sunny day. Pain, gentleness, and wisdom could be seen in her eyes, set into a weathered and wrinkled face. Happy to see Andrea, she was quick to invite them in and offered them food and coffee. She was Joe's housekeeper and assistant when he was in the settlement. Joe Doucette was a medical doctor who came out West after graduating from the University of Toronto. While at the University, Joe became a close friend of Alfred Shadd, the first black doctor in Saskatchewan. While visiting with Shadd in the Carrot River Valley, Joe recognized the need for doctors in the rapidly growing population of the Northwest Territories.

At that moment, Joe was at Blaine Lake setting the broken bones of William, "Scotty" Johnston and was not expected back home before dark. Joe's cabin had been built for Joe by the colony to show their appreciation for the compassion and concern he showed for the community. At least one day out of the week, Joe would appear to check on the health of the people, and never was more than one day's ride from the colony. It was in that cabin that Joe had saved Andrea's life. A drunk and jealous Scotsman had shot Beauchene in the stomach.

The woman in the garden had spread the word that Andrea was back. Most of the families within a mile gathered that evening to celebrate his return, except those who suspected him of tapping into their cookie jar. Metis need very little reason to celebrate. Welcoming home a respected and enjoyable friend like Andrea was reason enough. Blankets, shared by family and friends, were spread on the ground. Red River carts were parked back-to-back with planks between them for seating and tables. Two large kettles hung above a gentle fire that was releasing the aroma of a mouth-watering stew. It was still daylight, and the air was filled with music. Four fiddles, an harmonica, and flutes were playing polkas, quadrilles, and jigs. The dancers would only stop long enough to take a swig from jugs that were randomly located and go right back to their frolicking.

Lynes was both stimulated and mystified by the culture into which he was thrust. The music was like nothing he had ever heard, and the dancing much more aggressive than any dances he had ever attended. As Lynes was trying to figure out the nature of the dances, his train of thought was interrupted. Long flowing hair lightly touched his cheek. A young woman danced close by, deliberately tossing her hair at his face. Blask as a raven and nearly touching the ground, her hair floated in the air as she whirled wildly among the crowd of dancers. A bright red sash with long flowing ends hugged her tiny waist. The colorful blouse she wore was decorated with white beads that emphasized her pert breasts and wide shoulders. High cheek bones, heavy black eyebrows, a large nose, and wide lips watched over by huge dark eyes, somehow all came together to create a stunning face that could arouse lust in any man. Lynes watched her throw her hair in the face of another young man standing by a Red River cart. She jerked away and laughed when the young man reached out and grabbed her arm. The music continued unbroken as the sun began to set. Engrossed in the festivities, Lynes mind wandered away from his five o'clock rendezvous at the Presbyterian Church. His attention was on the dancing girl and the unbridled stamina she possessed. She never stopped dancing and exhausted every man, both young and old, who competed for her attention. When at last the music stopped, Lynes found Andrea and asked him if he knew who the beautiful girl was.

Andrea laughed a long, loud laugh, "Be careful Chiot; she could be one of mine."

Andrea's accepted trademark was that he jokingly laid claim to every child in the community (not without eliciting the ire of some of the more sober husbands). Andrea turned straight away and walked over and began talking to the young woman. Lynes, in near panic, felt hot blood rush to his ears as Andrea, holding the girl's hand, began walking in his direction. Lynes's eyes never left the dancer's face as Andrea with a mischievous twinkle in his eyes made the introductions.

"Renee, this is my Chiot, Lynes. Make him feel at home on our land. He hasn't met any of the young people here."

Andrea had no sooner finished introducing Lynes to Renee when he was taken away by a group of men who insisted on his participation.

Renee appeared to be indifferent to Lynes when she told him to follow her. She led him to a group of young men between the ages of sixteen and the early twenties. After introducing Lynes as a friend of Andrea, she turned and walked away. Lynes never took his eyes off her: his mesmerized stare drew laughter from the young men. One of the more verbal in the group, Rudy Macaslin, a short, stocky red-haired Scotsman, enthusiastically welcomed Lynes. Rudy's father had been on buffalo hunts with Andrea and so the father had told his son of the many exploits of Andrea Beauchene. Listening to the conversations among the young men amused Lynes, but his mind and eyes kept going back to Renee. Occasionally, their eyes would meet, and she would quickly look away. Then she was standing by the young man who had grabbed her arm when she was dancing. Lynes felt uneasy at the young man's stare. It was the stare of the alpha wolf challenging one of the lesser in the pack. Not wanting a confrontation, Lynes avoided the man's eyes.

The musicians began to take their places on the freight wagon stage. Brilliant colors filled the western sky as the sun disappeared below the horizon. Lanterns were hanging around the area, indicating the expectation that the party was going to be extended well into the evening. A small crowd gathered around a buckboard that had just arrived. Rudy steered Lynes's attention to the neatly dressed man getting out of the buckboard. There was pride in Rudy's voice when he spoke.

"That's our doctor, Joe Doucette. He's one helleva good man. Everybody here owes him in one way or another."

Doucette's compassion for his fellow man was unquestionable. While in medical school in Toronto, he stood by Alford Shadd whose rights were challenged as a black man in an all white environment. Dedicated to his work, Dr. Doucette demonstrated that the health of the poor was just as important to him as that of the privileged class. Sometimes such an attitude was to his detriment. A youthful face masked his age, but his steel gray eyes were those of a man of stern convictions. Without knowing why, Lynes felt privileged when he met Joe Doucette. Lynes and Andrea were invited to stay in the wigwam beside Joe's cabin, the same one frequently used by guests and patients of Dr. Doucette.

The flickering lights from the many lamps seemed to move to the rhythm of the music. In the darkness beyond the lamplights' glow, fireflies flashed in frantic efforts to find their mates. A full, silver moon began its journey in the heavens. The natural setting, gaiety, lively music, and the attraction Lyne had to Renee, ushered in a flood of emotions. His fight for survival for himself and his family in the wilderness gave him no time to experience such unbridled revelry. As he gazed around the crowd, Lynes searched for the beautiful girl with the flowing red sash. A flash of light and then darkness overcame Lynes. The young suitor whose stare Lynes had avoided previously, danced by and struck Lynes as if by accident, hitting him in the temple with an elbow. Dazed but still on his feet, Lynes turned to Rudy.

"What happened?"

Rudy looked around to those men who stood nearby to reinforce what he had seen. And then he turned to Lynes. "That son of a bitch did that on purpose!" He then explained what had happened.

A slow and calculated anger grew within Lynes, not so much because he had been assaulted but because the beauty and magic of the night had been stolen from him. Now, it was Lynes who had the stare of the alpha wolf. Lynes could see that the young man was watching him out of the corner of his eye, waiting for Lynes's reaction. The young trapper bided his time, waiting patiently for the offender to stop dancing. When the aggressor stopped to swig on a jug handed to him by one of his friends, Lynes was in his face.

"If you hit me on purpose, you are a coward. If it was an accident, you owe me an apology."

Looking into the young man's eyes, Lynes realized that his antagonist had stopped at too many jugs throughout the evening. When he took a swing at Lynes, he staggered backwards and would have fallen on his back if his friends had not caught him. The friends held the young man back as he struggled to free himself. Renee hurried to the altercation. It appeared to her that Lynes had knocked the young man into the arms of his friends. She stood in front of the drunken young dancer as if to protect him from Lynes. A smile crossed Lynes's face as he directed his words to Renee.

"I'll have a talk with your lover when he sobers up."

Lynes turned abruptly and stalked away. The magic of the night fled. Lynes's head throbbed as he walked dejectedly back to Joe Doucette's wigwam. It was late, and he had to rise early in the morning to take his place in the hiring line.

Andrea was sound asleep when Lynes saddled up Spade and rode off toward Prince Albert. He could see the glow of the mill burner in the distance when two figures, carrying a lantern, appeared in the darkness ahead of him. He approached the men with caution but felt secure upon the back of Spade. Lynes was pleasantly surprised to see it was Rudy and another young man he had met at the festivities the night before.

"Hello, Rudy. Hi, Billy. Are you going into Prince Albert?"

Rudy replied, "Ya. I'm going in to shovel shit, and Billy here will be shitting bricks." Seeing that he got a laugh out of Lynes, Rudy went on to explain that he worked at the Grand Union Livery Stables, and that Billy Fetters worked for the Red River Brick Company. Lynes apologized for not being able to walk along with them, but he wanted to be in the hiring line early.

Daylight began to break as Lynes rode down River Street. The train had just recently pulled into the station. Groups of people carrying suitcases and loaded backpacks followed behind wagons stacked with treasures from their homeland and homestead necessities. It was one of the many shiploads of immigrants from villages and towns in Europe and England escaping poverty. As Lynes rode through the throngs of people, he wondered how many of them would be in the hiring line tomorrow.

Frustrated by being rejected again at the hiring window, Lynes journeyed back into Prince Albert. His first stop was Lawyer Doak's office to see if there were any new developments concerning Ed. The rest of the day was spent seeking employment. With over 1,000 unemployed men in Prince Albert seeking employment in 1907, there was little chance that Lynes could land a job. Undaunted and filled with youthful optimism, he continued his search. As Lynes wandered throughout Prince Albert, it was inevitable that he would arrive at the Grand Union Livery Stables where Rudy worked. The large corral with four feeding stations held fourteen horses. The clean corral ground and the healthy condition of the horses were testimonial to the quality of the stables. Lynes found Rudy cleaning out one of the stalls in the horse barn.

"Hello, Rudy."

"Hello, Lynes. Did you get the job?"

"No. I've been all over town trying to find work but haven't had any luck. Do you think they might need help here?"

"Old Sam always needs help. However, he don't pay no more than ten cents an hour for regular help." (Labor wages in Prince Albert in 1907 were fifteen to eighteen cents per hour.) "People don't stay long."

"I get a bit more 'cause he trusts me to run the place when he ain't around. I might be able to talk him into putting you on. He ain't here right now, but when he shows up, I'll talk to him."

It was nearing five o'clock, and Lynes was hoping he would find Monique waiting for him at the church. "Thanks a lot, Rudy. I have to meet someone at the Presbyterian Church right now. I don't know how long I'll be. I'll be back as soon as I can."

Lynes closed his eyes as he touched the ornate church door. 'Let her be here' kept racing through his head as the door slowly opened. He stepped into the church and looked in the direction where he had first met Monique. There, sitting beside Monique, was the young minister, Colin Young. Lynes felt frustration and disappointment when he saw someone else sitting where he should be. He wanted Monique to be with him only and resented the presence of the Reverend Young. Lynes walked out of the church. As he climbed astride Spade, he had a strange feeling. It was as if he had lost something precious. He was about to ride away when he heard the voice of the Reverend.

"Lynes! Lynes! Where are you going? We want to talk to you."

Lynes twisted around to see the Reverend Young standing on the church steps and Monique walking out of the doors behind him. She called out his name.

"Lynes, mon amour!"

All of the confusing emotions Lynes had felt just moments before melted away. "Mon amour" turned his world into ecstasy.

Monique raced down the church steps and grabbed Lynes by the hand. She longed to embrace him in her arms, but the Victorian conventions of the day prohibited such behavior from a young lady.

Lynes never said a word as she led him into the church, with Reverend following behind. Colin stood in front of the couple, expecting them to give him their attention; instead, their eyes never left each other's. Monique held both of Lynes's hands in hers. He was aroused by her fragrance and beauty as she pulled him close to her body. Her eyes sparkled like blue diamonds, her luscious lips but inches from his. Her voice was almost a whisper.

"I waited so long to see you, mon amour."

The Reverend Young was astounded by the impropriety of Monique's public display. He felt it was his responsibility as a man of the cloth to intervene. His words were directed to Lynes.

"Monique has told me about your friend, Lynes. She and I had quite a long talk yesterday. There are some things you should know. I have to talk to you."

As Colin spoke, Lynes and Monique remained locked in each other's gaze. The young minister wasn't accustomed to being ignored. The next time he spoke, it was with authority, urgency, and volume. It was the voice he used delivering a sermon.

"Children! Children!" (The two lovers looked up at Colin's second 'Children.' "TThis is a house of worship. It is not a house of pleasures of the flesh. Lynes, it is important that I have a talk with you. I know all about your friend in jail, and I know Monique's father is …"

Colin never got to finish his sentence. Lynes jumped to his feet and faced Colin Young. The Reverend's interference and insistence exasperated him. Lynes interrupted Colin's tirade to stop him from what he perceived to be none of Colin's business. He couldn't contain his words.

"Just hold on there, preacher! If you want to have a talk with me, we'll have that talk I came here to see Monique, not to get preached to."

With that admonition, Lynes reached down and grasped Monique's hand and raised her to her feet. There was no resistance from Monique. Colin's protests fell upon deaf ears as Lynes and Monique left the church.

Lynes was surprised at how light the young girl was as he lifted her onto the beautifully ornate moose horn saddle. Monique was aroused by the gentle strength in Lynes's hands that encircled her tiny waist. Lynes threw himself up onto Spade's rump, his arms surrounding Monique as they disappeared into the trees not far behind the church.

Monique remained waiting on Spade's back as Lynes dismounted and spread the soft beaver skin blanket that was his constant companion upon the earth. He gently lifted Monique from the horse and knelt down upon the blanket with her in his arms. As their lips met, their embrace turned to tender exploration. The salty, sweet taste of Monique's breast brought Lynes to an intensity that bordered on insanity. He was brought back to harsh reality when he heard a voice that seemed to come from beyond this world.

"Lynes, mon bien-aime. Please stop. We cannot do this."

Struggling to resist Monique's plea, Lynes tasted the delicate hard nipples of her breast. Savoring the sweetness of her warm, soft skin, Lynes directed his kisses upwards to end their journey mixed with the nectar from her trembling lips. Like a ship in uncharted waters, Lynes had explored into the unknown. He loathed ending the voyage as his loins ached with the heat of his passion. Fighting back his instinct to have her for his pleasure, Lynes lifted her lacy blouse over her soft, white shoulders. Then he whispered in Monique's ear. "Just one more kiss."

The cooling off period lasted a long time as they held each other. Each was lost in his/her own thoughts about what had just occurred. At last, Monique broke the long silence.

"Are you going to see the Reverend?"

Lynes was speechless. After what had just happened, how could she bring up anything except the intensity of the moment and the love he had expressed? He was duly perplexed as she continued her line of thought.

"He seemed very concerned when I told him about your friend. Maybe he could help. He did say that it was important that he talk with you." Alluding to Colin was Monique's way of defusing the deep passion she had just experienced.

Recalling his prior exchange with Colin, Lynes responded, "We'll have that talk." Lynes was bound to keep his word. After vowing to see each other again, Monique and Lynes parted. Lynes rode nervously back to the Presbyterian Church.

Colin was sitting in a pew in front of the pulpit going through papers when Lynes approached. The minister's attention remained fixed on the papers. Lynes was about to turn and leave when Colin looked up and with a smile said, "Well, hello, Lynes. I'm glad you could find your way back."

To Lynes, Colin had become an adversary when he protested Monique's leaving the church. Cautious not to show his true feelings, Lynes acted calm and reserved. He wanted to avoid any conversation alluding to Monique and him leaving the church against the minister's wishes. That topic, he feared, would elicit a confrontation.

"You said that Monique told you about my friend, Ed. What is it about my friend that you want to discuss?"

Colin was more concerned about protecting Monique than he was about the fate of Lynes's friend. The rules of relationships between young men and women in 1907 forbid private meetings without a charperone. Such a meeting would ruin a young woman's reputation. Young men who violated that social more were subject to public criticism, and it was culturally acceptable for physical punishment to be wrought by the father or brother of the involved young woman. Metis were considered a sub culture by the clergy and government, and Colin knew that Lynes was in grave danger if Monique's father got wind of the pair's trysts at the church.

"I'll do what I can to help your friend, but it is more important that you understand why you cannot keep seeing your friend, Monique."

Lynes grew angry at these words, but they did not come as a surprise. He waited for Colin to tell him something he didn't already know. After telling Colin to mind his own business, Lynes left the church, unaware of the danger he was in.

The only person at the Grand Union Livery Stables was a homeless man. The owner, Sam, profited by charging the vagrant twenty cents a night for shelter, and also acquired the benefit of having the man as a free night watchman. Sam Donaldson was notorious as a miser and yet a shrewd horse trader. Lynes was anxious to find out if Rudy had been able to talk Sam into putting him to work. There was a lot on Lynes's mind as he rode out of town in the direction of the Metis village. Tomorrow, he would be allowed to visit with Ed DeGrace and maybe get a job at the mill or stables. Hopefully, he would also be able to catch Monique on her way to the church. Colin's warning kept coming back to him. He did not want the preacher to see Monique and him together.

The moon was full and its color matched the lamplights that shone through the windows as Lynes rode into the village. He found Rudy and Bill sitting in front of their home, having their last pipe before going to bed. Rudy looked up at Lynes.

"That's one hell of a nice horse. Old Sam is gonna want to get his hands on him. Did ya get your business taken care of in Prince Albert?"

There was a smile on Lynes's face when he gave Rudy his answer, "Almost."

It was customary in the West to stay mounted when visiting unless you were invited to stay. Bill spoke up.

"Get off that glue factory and sit a spell. We were about to hit the rack, but you and old Andrea showing up gives us somethin' to talk about. Gotta tell ya what happened last night after you disappeared. That guy you knocked on his ass was staggering all over the place lookin' to get his ass kicked again. Every time he swung at somebody, he'd fall on his ass. Musta fallen twenty times last night. And then the dangest thing you ever did see happened. Andrea musta been dancing with the wrong Indian. Her husband, just a little feller, jumped upon Andrea's back and started chewing on his ear. Then Andrea's dog, I think his name is Wolf, jumped up and grabbed the feller by his ass. Funniest thing I ever did see. That feller hangin' off Andrea's back and that dog hangin' off that feller. Laughed 'til I cried."

Although he was concerned about Andrea's ear, Lynes couldn't keep from laughing along with Rudy and Bill. Lynes was excited to learn that he could go to work at the stables any time he wanted. This would be his first job, although it only paid seven cents an hour. Lynes recalled the long flowing hair of the beautiful Renee when Bill told him that she was looking for him and appeared to have an interest in him after the big shindig. The three young men were enjoying their pipes and conversation when Rudy's father interrupted them.

"Let's go to bed boys; we got an early morning start."

Lynes accompanied his friends into Prince Albert the next morning. The Red River cart was loaded with produce and products destined for the markets in Prince Albert and outlying settlements. Rudy's father would distribute the load after dropping Rudy and Bill off at their jobs.

The hiring line was long as usual, and Lynes was eager to get to the window. He wished he had left the settlement earlier or ridden on ahead of his friends. It was the practice for the hiring boss to yell out, "Hiring line closed," after filling the needed positions. Lynes was relieved and surprised that he made it to the window.

"Lynes, you will be going to work on the night shift, feeding slip. Go to the store and get your boots."

The hiring boss wasn't surprised by the look of confusion on the young trapper's face. His card said he was an interpreter and hunter, not a mill worker. The boss told Lynes where to go to find the boom boss and get filled in on what his job was going to be. Lynes was relieved to see that feeding the logs into the mill was a simple job. Thrusting the fifteen foot long pike pole into a log, giving it a twist, and pulling the log on to the slip (a chain that pulls the log into the mill) was right up his alley. His next stop was the company store to get his caulked boots (boots with studs on the soles for traction). After signing an agreement that everything he bought at the store would be taken out of his pay, Lynes walked out admiring his first store bought boots. It would only take him twenty -four hours of feeding slip to pay for his boots.

A feeling of despair suddenly came over Lynes as he again walked into visit Ed in jail. On the way to Ed's cell, Peter Forsyth, the turnkey, lightened his depressiona a bit.

"That friend of yours must know somebody upstairs. We been treating him like this is a first class hotel."

In 1907, the Canadian prison system policy, as it was in the United States, was to punish prisoners. The turnkey sounded annoyed that he had to treat a prisoner humanely. Peter Forsyth opened Ed's door.

"Give me a holler when you're done."

A chill gripped Lynes when he entered the cell. The warmth of the summer couldn't penetrate the prison walls. He got an eerie feeling when Peter closed the cell door behing him and turned the key in the lock. Lynes, remembering the trapped snow white Arctic fox he had released from the box, became conscious of his own momentary panic. That tension was relieved when Ed told him to sit down.

"Sit down and make yourself at home."

Ed moved an empty food bowl from the solid iron bed that hung from the wall, giving Lynes room to sit. A one-inch thick, bug-infested mat was all that covered the bunk. It was not designed for comfort. In the far corner of the cell sat a potty; a water bucket sat near the cell door. A light bulb hanging in the corridor barely pierced the darkness. An atmosphere of depression and gloom surrounded the quarters. Lynes wondered how the turnkey could think this was anything like a first class hotel.

Ed placed his arm around Lynes and pulling him close to him, shoulder to shoulder, said, "Mon ami, tell me how you have been?"

Lynes started out by telling Ed that he had seen Algernon Doak the day before, and that all the attorney would say was that he was working on Ed's case. Omitting the tumultuous events of their meeting, Lynes told Ed that he had met a minister who said that he would do what he could to help him. Lynes went on to tell Ed about Andrea introducing him to the Metis village and his good luck at finding two jobs in one day.

Ed was especially pleased that Pique (Spade) was being well taken care of. After running out of things to say, Lynes turned the conversation to Ed.

"You sure look a lot better than you did the last time I saw you. What do they have you doing?"

"Well, for the first couple of days they had me working in a coal mine. That's when you saw me. Now, I've got a cushy job over at the Mounty headquarters sweeping the floors and pouring coffee. Beats the hell out of the coal mines. They treat me pretty good over there."

After over an hour, everything that could be said was said. The two men sat in silence on the edge of the bunk, each unwilling to say good-by. At last, the silence was broken. Unexpectedly to Lynes, Ed stood up and hollered out.

"Hey, let my friend out of here."

Lynes was shivering from the chill in the jail cell as Peter led him down the prison corridor. Concerned about Ed's comfort, he asked if he could take his friend a blanket. Peter's response was that anything pertaining to Ed DeGrace had to be cleared through the Royal Northwest Mounted Police. Lynes remembered Sgt. Major Marshall saying he was going to look in on Ed. He wondered if the Sgt. Major had anything to do with Ed's getting a cushy job. This would be a good time to take Marshall up on his invitation to drop on by.

Marshall concealed how pleased he was to see Lynes. He tried to hide his pleasure, but when he looked up at Lynes, every line in his rugged face told the story. It never happened that anyone walked up to his desk just to visit. He didn't expect Lynes's visit to be any different.

"How are you doing, Lynes? What can I do for you?"

Suspecting that it was Marshall who made life easier for Ed, Lynes stated how relieved he was that Ed was doing so much better than he was at his last visit.

Although Marshall held Reil's rebels in contempt, he did not agree with the government's inhumane treatment of prisoners, regardless of the crime. As an idealistic youth, he had made the epic journey West to protect the Indians from the white settlers' abuse. But he was soon to discover that he was the judge and jury in the wild Northwest, as well as teacher and arbitrator. Few who knew him would challenge his authority, including the prison warden. He was quick to give Lynes permission to give Ed a blanket, not only for humanitarian reasons, but because he enjoyed annoying the abusive warden.

"You betcha, Lynes. I'll see that Ed geta a blanket."

"That would be good. I want to give him mine. It is a blanket my mother made. I know it will keep him warm." While Lynes went outside to untie the soft beaver skin blanket from the saddle, Marshall thought how fortunate Ed was to have such a devoted friend.

It was near noon when Lynes rode up to the Grand Union Livery Stables. Rudy pointed Sam out to Lynes. Sam was trying to sell a matched team of horses to a newly arrived settler. Both bay horses were seventeen hands high with identical markings. The trader sold the settler one horse for $35.00. The other, he sold for $32.00. He said it was because he didn't think the $32.00 horse looked too good. The settler drove off with a perfectly matched team, unaware that one of the horses was blind. Such a man was Sam Donaldson. Sam spied Lynes standing beside Spade and immediately began to speculate on how he was going to gain ownership of that magnificent horseflesh. Gaining Lynes's confidence and friendship was his first calculated step.

"By Golly, you must be Rudy's friend. He told me you had a fine horse. Looks like you do a fine job taking care of him, too. You can put him in the corral and start working anytime you want. Rudy will show you what needs to be done."

Lynes led Spade into the corral and started to work at his first job. The stables closed the barn doors at eight o'clock. Lynes calculated that he had earned sixty-three cents. His visit with Ed and his job at the mill in just four more hours would end an almost perfect day. The only disappointment was that he didn't get to see his lovely Monique. His twelve-hour shift at the mill would end at noon tomorrow, and somehow, someway, he would find a way to see the love of his life.

The midnight whistle blew and Lynes took his place on the catwalk. His caulked boots dug into the walk as he leaned back slowly pulling the heavy log into the slip. He gave the pike pole a twist, freeing it from the log, and then tossed it out again into another log. Another twist on the pole, and again straining backwards to feed the log into the slip and so the night wore on. And then the inevitable happened. As Lynes leaned back, his full weight against the pole, the twisted tip pulled loose from the log. Lynes fell backwards off the narrow catwalk and plunged into the icy North Saskatchewan River.

With the exception of his caulked boots, Lynes was dry by the time the noon whistle blew. He was glad to get the boots off his wrinkled feet as he rode back to Prince Albert on a lumber wagon. Spade walked up to Lynes and nuzzled him a warm welcome when he arrived back at the Grand Union Stables. He gave Spade a half dissolved sugar cube out of his beaded pouch. From within the barn, Sam watched the relationship between Lynes and Spade. Slowly, he walked out of the barn and approached Lynes.

"I see you left your horse here last night, and he's been here all day. I'm going to have to charge you board for your horse." Lynes was about to learn what a tightwad Sam Donaldson really was.

"How much do I owe you?"

"Two dollars for the time he spent in my corral while you were gone. I won't charge you for corral time while you are here working. If you want to put him up for the night, inside the barn, it'll be another three dollars."

A large sign with big red letters hung on the barn door. It advertised the quality, security, and care given to horses boarded at the Grand Union Stables. A one-foot square sign in small black letters was attached to the corral gate. It relieved the proprietor of responsibility if a horse in the corral was stolen at night. When Rudy brought the sign to Lynes's attention, he felt guilty for leaving Spade in the corral the previous night. For Spade's safety, Rudy offered to take care of him at night. Rudy would have transportation to and from work, and Spade would have shelter at night. Noticing the condition of Rudy's father's horse, Lynes felt Ed's horse would be well taken care of and out of the reach of Sam Donaldson.

It was nearing five o'clock. Hoping to catch Monique before she arrived at church, Lynes saddled up Spade. When he arrived, he peeked inside the church to see if Monique was already there. To his chagrin, Monique's father, Colin Young, and two large men were lying in wait. Lynes didn't know what to expect, but he knew that whatever it was, he wasn't going to like it. His first instinct was to flee, but he was stopped by Colin's words.

"Wait, Lynes, we just want to talk with you."

In an effort to hide his anxiety, Lynes cautiously approached the four men. Colin started to speak, but he was interrupted by Monique's father whose tone of voice was angry and threatening.

"Now, listen you damn half-breed! I told you to stay away from my daughter. You see those two men there? (He pointed at the two large men, one holding a whip.) I'd be within my rights to have 'em horsewhip the skin off your ass. That's why they're here. But the Reverend here talked me into giving you a choice. He told me all about your friend in jail. I'll get your no-good, worthless friend out of jail, and you stay the hell away from my daughter! I think I'd get better results giving you a good horse whipping...What do you say?"

Lynes looked into Treaudeaux's eyes. They burned with hatred as he waited for Lynes to respond.

"I'll stay away from your daughter." Lynes had to choke out his words.

"You damn well better!" Treaudeaux nodded to the large man wielding the whip.

Lynes felt a burning sensation across his face as the braided leather whip was snatched from around his head. As Lynes held his bleeding face in his hands, Treaudeaux's angry voice boomed in his ears.

"That's just a sample of what you'll get if you ever see my daughter again."

Still holding his wounded face in his hands, Lynes heard the three men leave the church. He winced when he felt a hand on his shoulder. Expecting to see blood, Lynes slowly lowered his hands. Colin stood in front of him. His face and voice were filled with compassion.

"I'm sorry, Lynes; I didn't want that to happen."

Lynes cast Colin's hand from his shoulder. Feeling a burning hatred toward Treaudeaux, Lynes left the church. A kind of hatred he had never felt before permeated his whole being. The pain in his face dwarfed the agony he felt from the loss of the woman he loved. The thought that he might never see Monique again was more excruciating than the welt that marked his face. He would have welcomed the whipping if it meant that they could still be together. Fighting back a feeling of guilt, Lynes wondered if Ed's freedom was worth the price he had personally paid.

Rudy looked surprised when he saw the red welt across Lynes's face. "What the hell happened to you? Stay right there." Rudy grabbed a can of salve used to treat horse wounds and smeared it on the welt.

Lynes was not in the mood for a long conversation. He said that he didn't want to talk about it and then busied himself cleaning the stalls at the stables. When eight o'clock rolled around, Rudy saddled up Spade and left for the village. Lynes curled up in the hay under a horse blanket. There was no rest. He was haunted by the face of Treaudeaux, twisted with anger and hatred. When Satuday finally dawned, Lynes was thankful it was the last workday at the mill.

He felt the pike pole slide through his hand, its target a Jack pine log. And then a THUNK, a twist and pull, over and over again. The boring, simple task gave Lynes time to sort out his priorities. No longer was the cold steel point of the pike pole thrusting into the heart of Treaudeaux. As the darkness of the night gradually gave way to the warmth of the sun, so, too, did the madness of yesterday fade into the light of reason. Lamenting the agreement that he had made with Treaudeaux, Lynes trusted the deal would be done. The ride on the lumber wagon carrying Lynes back to Prince Albert seemed to take forever. Lynes was eager to see Ed a free man again.

Marshall's face lit up when Lynes walked into his office. The older man wanted to see the look on the young trapper's face when he told him that Ed was released. However, the Mountie's expression changed at the sight of the red welt across Lynes's face.

"My God! What happened to you?"

Lynes had been convinced by Colin Young that by courting the lovely Monique, he, a Metis, had broken the white man's law. Fearful of what Marshall might do, Lynes attributed his injury to an accident at the Grand Union Stables. Marshall was puzzled by the stern, almost angry look of resolve by Lynes when he told him that Ed had been released. There were questions in Marshall's mind when Lynes left his office. Anger and resolve were not the proper reaction to good news. Lynes's behavior prompted Marshall to question if there was a connection between Judge Prendergast's dropping the charges against Ed and the welt across Lynes's face. He had no doubt that he would ferret out the answer.

Lynes found Ed at the Grand Union Stables. Rudy had already informed Ed that Lynes was injured but wouldn't talk about it. Ed and Lynes had a heated discussion about the injury, but Lynes refused to tell him what had happened. Ed was holding his Henry in his hand, and Lynes was afraid Ed would use it. With Monique in mind, Lynes promised himself that one day when they were passing the stick during their ritual observances, he would tell the whole story.

Ed wanted to show his gratitude to his youthful, loyal benefactor. "I'm gonna' take back my horse, but I ain't gonna' leave you afoot. You just pick out any horse in this corral, and she's yours."

Lynes hesitated. He expected no reward for his endeavors. Throughout Lynes's ordeal, Ed's freedom was the only reward he sought. Fully aware of the trials and hardships experienced by a fur trapper in order to make a dollar, Lynes refused Ed's generous offer. Unwilling to accept Lynes's rebuff, Ed climbed into the corral and began inspecting the horses. Ed chose a large, bay stallion. It was obvious that the horse was from Cheval Canadian stock, a breed that developed from horses introduced into Canada by the King of France in the 1600s. This breed was affectionately called, "The Little Iron Horse." The arched thick neck and long wavy mane and tail gave the stallion an almost royal stature. This horse stood as tall as Pique, and its cannon girth gave Ed the confidence that Lynes would have a sure-footed horse with outstanding endurance. Ed called out to Sam McDonald.

"Throw a saddle on this piece of meat. Let's see how she rides."

Sam ignored Ed's request and began pointing out all of the quality features that made him stand out from the other horses in his corral. Ed had no doubt of the stallion's soundness when he examined him and watched him move around among the other horses in the corral. An Indian, who appeared to be drunk, had sold the young stallion to Sam for $2.00 and a fifth of whiskey. In his haste to skin the Indian out of the horse, the trader had failed to check out if the horse could be ridden. After numerous attempts to break the stallion on his own and failing, Sam had been contemplating sending the beast to the rendering plant. Eager to get rid of the hay burner, and to hide the fact that he couldn't be ridden, Sam continued to give his sales pitch, hoping Ed would make the same mistake that he did.

"Hell, there ain't no use for that. Since the youngster works for me, and I know he'll take good care of him, I'll give you the horse for $300 even. A horse like that's worth $500 easy." Being an expert horse trader, Sam had perfected his mannerisms, enabling him to lure his prey into haggling. As was customary for horse traders, Ed, considering himself a horse trader in his own right, came back with what he thought was an unrealistically low figure.

"I'll give you a $100, and you throw in a saddle and blanket."

Sam threw his hands to his face and bent over like he had been kicked in the guts. Shaking his head in disgust and looking directly into Ed's eyes, he acted as if he were resigned to the inevitable. Satisfied that he had convinced Ed that he was getting a great bargain, the trader replied, "Oh! What the hell! You're giving the horse away as a gift, and I can see the youngster wants the animal. Come on into the office, and I'll make out the papers."

The stallion's ears perked up as Lynes walked toward him, holding the hackamore behind his back. As Lynes edged closer, the stallion's bright, grandmotherly gentle eyes blinked inquisitively. Taking care to avoid direct eye contact when he slowly approached the horse, Lynes spoke softly as his freehand gently stroked the stallion's throat. There was no fear in the animal's alert eyes, only a subtle shudder of his withers as the young man slipped the hackamore over his nose. The horse stood, calm and indifferent, when the blanket was placed on his back, but at the instant Ed touched his back with the saddle, the stallion erupted like a volcano. The saddle was thrown fifteen feet into the air while the stallion chased Ed and Lynes out of the corral.

Outside the corral, Sam was patting himself on the back; Ed was questioning his own competence as a horse trader; and Lynes was wishing that he had asked Rudy about the horse. The victorious stallion, with a serene, innocent expression upon his face, stood calmly gazing at the two men. The road to the Metis village found Ed riding Pique and carrying a saddle, and close behind, Rudy, Bill, and Lynes following. Lynes was leading his handsome Canadian bay, Cheval.

Dr. Joe Doucette gave Lynes a jar of ointment that he said would relieve the stinging and minimize the scar on his face. He complimented Rudy for his quick action of applying Jelstrom's Oak Bark Horse Salve on the welt. He and Rudy had both seen the remarkable healing power of the product. Joe chuckled when he wryly said, "Maybe that's what I should have used on Andrea's ear."

Lynes felt more comfortable in the Metis village than he did in Prince Albert. Not only did almost everyone speak his tongue, but also they were a lot more friendly than the city folk. The invitation by Rudy's father that he move in with him, Rudy, and Bill was very much appreciated. That evening, Lynes was to learn just how altruistic Rudy's father was.

Although Rudy was much shorter than Bill and sported flaming red hair, and Bill much taller with black curly hair and steel blue eyes, Lynes assumed the two were brothers. He soon learned that Bill was one of the many children England sent around the world to populate its vast British Empire. Twenty-five per cent of the world landmass in the early 1900s was under the British flag. However, the massive wealth generated by England in the Industrial Age did not trickle down to the hungry, homeless children on the streets of London and other industrial cities. These waifs were called "Home Children," "Waifs and Strays," and "Orphans," such as "St. Vincent's Orphans."

There were at least fifty organizations in England shipping children ages four to fifteen to Canada and other countries. Some were chattel. Some were indentured servants until the age of eighteen. Others were farm workers, industrial workers, and apprentices. Children as young as nine years old worked in the coal mines, Canada's largest industry in the 1900s. Bill was only fours years old when he was taken from his sixteen-year-old brother off the streets of Liverpool. His brother was taken to a workhouse while Bill was put on a steamship, <u>Sarmatian</u>, and sent to Canada as an indentured servant. At nine years old, Bill ran away from the abusive home he had been taken to in Manitoba. He hopped a train and rode it to the end of the line, Prince Albert. Rudy and his father were in the process of taking a load of produce into the city when they saw the runaway jump off the train. Dirty and hungry, Bill ran to catch up to the Red River cart and asked if he could spare something to eat off the cart. Rudy's father answered the boy,

"You look like you need more than an ear of corn. Hop on up here."

From that day on, Rudy and Bill were brothers. Rudy's father had lost his wife when she gave birth to his son. Of necessity, he assumed the role of mother and father, giving Rudy the love and tenderness he had known from Rudy's mother, and all that he knew it took to be a good man. As much as he loved Rudy, he showed no favoritism between Rudy and Bill, and now he was willing to take another fledgling under his wing. Lynes dropped off to sleep that night, comfortable in feeling that he was a part of Rudy's family.

"WHEN I GET UP, EVERYBODY GETS UP!"

Rudy and Bill had heard that comman before. It was Sunday morning, and Rudy's father playfully hollered out every Sunday morning to wake his sons for church. It was also customary for him to have a hearty breakfast ready by the time they got up. Lynes, awakened, his senses filled with the tantalizing aroma of pancakes cooking, buffalo bacon frying, and coffe simmering on the stove.

After breakfast, Bill harnessed Dumont to pick up their neighbors for church. Three Red River carts loaded with families lumbered over the deep-rutted road to Prince Albert. Lynes noted that the raven-haired Renee was riding in the cart behind him.

When the group arrived at the Catholic mission built by Father Andre twenty-five years earlier, they gathered outside and then entered the mission together. The humble building was not built to handle the booming population of Prince Albert. In five years, a massive cathedral would be built where the humble mission now stood. There wasn't room to seat all the worshipers so Lynes stood in the back of the mission along with the younger people from the village. Behind Lynes stood Renee, the lovely Metis maiden. Throughout the service, Lynes could feel the girl's breasts occasionally rub against his back. He wondered if she was doing it on purpose or if it was by accident. In either case, he welcomed the sensation. Lynes's thoughts wandered back to the firm breasts of Monique and the taste and fragrance of her body. In his prayers he thanked God for having Monique as a part of his life and for giving him the opportunity to free Ed DeGrace. Prayer was important to Lynes as he had been instructed by the priests on the Little Red River, and by his Grandfather, Big Hand, and his mother, Margarette. Nonetheless, it was hard to concentrate on prayer with Renee rubbing her breasts on his back.

Ed DeGrace stated he was in a hurry to get back to his village on the Little Red River. Andrea decided to stay on in the care of Joe Doucette until his injured ear grew back on. Ed promised Lynes that he would tell Pierre and Margarette that their son was in good hands. The last words that he spoke to Lynes were, "The next time I see you, you better be riding that bay."

The days grew longer for Lynes as he fed the slip and worked with Rudy at the Grand Union Stables. In his zeal to prosper, Lynes gave every waking hour to his labor. Physically exhausted by the end of the week, he would trade his bed in the barn for the comfort of Rudy's and his father's cabin. The McCaslin family left Lynes to sleep on Monday mornings, giving him a chance to catch up on the sleep he lost during the week. When he awakened on his fourth Monday morning at Rudy's, everything was as it had been on previous Mondays, with one exception. Folded neatly on the foot of Lynes's bed in the quiet, empty cabin lay a well-made wool shirt. The black and red plaid colors caught his eye immediately. Nice shirt, he thought. Someone must have laid it there and forgot to put it away.

As he did every Monday morning, Lynes prepared himself a hearty breakfast, visited his "Little Iron Horse," and then made his way to work at the stables. On his way out of the village, he passed the garden where Renee was weeding the rows. Acknowledging her presence, Lynes nodded his head as was his custom. She stood up and faced him. For a moment, Lynes was bewildered by her response to his attention. Jet black hair hung in braids over her shoulders. She threw back her head, the movement accentuating her ample breasts. Her voluptuous body turned from side to side in an effort to tease Lynes's masculine desires. The seductive body language and the playful shaping of her lips as if to kiss him from afar did just what Renee intended. However, Lynes just nodded and continued on as if he did not recognize her bold and provocative response. But in his mind's eye, Lynes vividly recalled the night Renee captured his passion as he watched her dance. He was half way to Prince Albert before he could get his mind off the wild and ravishing beauty.

The young Mountie who had been instructed to keep an eye on Lynes, walked up to Sgt. Major Marshall's desk who questioned him, "I haven't heard anything about that trapper kid. Is he still in town?"

"Yes, sir, he works and sleeps in the barn at the Grand Union Stables, and also works at the Prince Albert Lumber Mill on the night shift. I haven't seen him wandering around town getting into trouble."

Marshall was thinking of the glaring welt on Lynes's face. "The last time I saw him he had an ugly welt on his face. Keep your ears open; you might be able to find out what happened."

An order given by a Sgt. Major in the Royal Northwest Mounted Police was not to be taken lightly. The young Mountie registered that his superior expected a report on his desk, documenting every phase of his investigation. A Royal Mountie had to accurately document everything while he was on patrol, even the weather. (One patrol could cover as much as 900 miles of territory.) In good faith, the RNWMP negotiated the treaties with the First Nation's people. The men kept order in the settlements as well as teaching the people how to farm.

They also delivered the mail, fought prairie fires, sickness, and disease, and protected the First Nation's people from alcohol and mistreatment from the settlers. The mounted police's fairness and professionalism gave them the well-earned respect from both the Indian and the white man. The young Mountie followed in his father's tradition. His father had been sent out West in 1874 to bring law to Saskatchewan, and the son was there to maintain it now. The report on his investigation regarding Lynes was laid on the Marshall's desk three days later and read as follows:

"I started my investigation at the Grand Union Stables, questioning Rudy McCaslin, the stable boy who works with Lynes. The only thing he could tell me is that Lynes had an altercation at the Presbyterian Church. He could tell me nothing more. I followed up by going immediately to the church to find out if Reverend Colin Young knew anything about the matter. He told me that Lynes and a young woman, Monique Treaudeaux, had been meeting in his church for several weeks, and that he knew that her father, Robert Treaudeaux, had forbidden them to see each other. The minister explained that it was his duty to let Treaudeaux know the two were meeting so he could protect his daughter from the half-breed. He said Treaudeaux and two other men came to his church and waited for Lynes to show up. When Lynes appeared, Mr. Treaudeaux persuaded Lynes to stay away from his daughter. One of the three men with Treaudeaux struck Lynes with a whip. Colin said that he did not expect violence in his church, and that he would have stopped it had he known it was going to happen. He also said that he did not know the man who used the whip on Lynes. After that, I went to the Prince Albert Hotel where Robert Treaudeaux and his daughter were staying. Treaudeaux was not there, but I did meet with Monique who seemed distraught that she had not seen Lynes for more than a month. The following morning, I went to the office of McKay and Adams to meet with Mr. Treaudeaux. Treaudeaux stated that he brought the two men with him for protection, and that he never told his companion to strike Lynes. When I asked him who the man was with the whip, he told me it was Steven Howe, a camp construction boss for the Prince Albert Lumber Company. I then went to the lumber company to find Steven Howe. I was told that Howe was building a camp on the White Gull

River and that he would be back in Prince Albert in about forty-five days. My conclusion is that Steven Howe may be charged with assult."

After reading the report, Marshall's suspicions were confirmed: the welt on Lynes's face and Ed's release were related. Reflecting upon James McKay's influence, Marshall realized that pressing charges against Steven Howe would be futile. "Having met Lynes's father and Ed DeGrace, I have a feeling that Steven Howe may get a taste of native justice."

The clerk at the company store was surprised when Lynes exchanged his script for real money. It wasn't often that he counted out $43.00 to a mill worker. By the end of the month, it was expected that an employee owed more money than he had earned. This was Lynes's fifth week at the mill. In spite of that, the company held back a week's pay on the first month's check. Lynes's boots were now paid for, along with the sugar, coffee, and tobacco that he had purchased for his bunkmates.

As he crossed the bridge into Prince Albert, Lynes's eagerness to see his horse and friends was overcome by his burning desire to see Monique. He thought, "Maybe if I walk around the town, I will at least get a glimpse of her. Just to see her one more time would complete my life." Then, Lynes was struck with anxiety, "What if she left town? She said she was just here visiting.'

Lynes's thoughts were on a rollercoaster. Torn between emotions and reason, he subconsciously began walking toward the church. Above the noise and clamor of busy River Street, Lynes heard someone call out his name.

"Lynes!"

When he turned in the direction of the voice, he saw the young Mountie striding toward him. "Monsieur Mountie, what can I do for you?"

"You can come with me. My Sgt. Major wants to talk to you."

Lynes thought that the white man's rules were that a Metis could not have a relationship with a white woman. As the two men walked to the Mountie headquarters, Lynes wondered what the punishment would be if Marshall knew that he had been seeing Monique, or if he had broken some other rule. He inquired of the young Mountie, "Monsieur Mountie, have I done something wrong?"

"Not that I know of," the young Mountie replied.

It was obvious to Marshall that Lynes was apprehensive when the young Mountie brought him to his desk. "Well, Lynes, I think we've got a problem here. It's against the law to give a law enforcement officer false information."

Lynes could feel his heart race as he pictured himself in Ed's jail cell. Marshall continued, "I found out how you got that welt across your face. Looks like it healed up real well. Did you tell Ed DeGrace what happened?"

"No."

"I hope you're telling me the truth. I'm compelled to tell you if anything happens to the fellow who used the whip on you, I'm going to assume that Ed got to him for revenge, and your friend will be back in here sweeping floors again. If anything is going to be done, I'll do it."

Lynes wasn't concerned about Ed's getting revenge; he was dreading what Marshall was going to do to him for courting Monique. "I gave her father my word. I won't see her again."

"I know you won't; they went back East two days ago. I'm going to release you now, but I want you to understand that when I ask you a question, I want the truth. Do you understand?"

Lynes shook his head "Yes," and Marshall smiled inside at the youthful and innocent look on his face. He had seen that look so many times on his son's face. "Now get out of here."

Relieved that he wasn't going to jail, Lynes headed for the door. He was half way there when the Marshall's voice stopped him. "If you run into trouble, I want you to come here first."

Still facing the door, Lynes glanced back at Marshall, shook his head "Yes" and hurried out the door. There was a sadness in Lynes as he walked away from the NWMP headquarters. A sadness that he would never see Monique again and yet relief that he would not be tempted by his love for her to seek her out again in Prince Albert. He thought, maybe I will see her again if Kice Manito wills it.

When Lynes reached the settlenent, he found Andrea sitting on Joe Doucette's porch, Wolf at his feet and a backpack by his side.

"Going some place? Lynes knew what Andrea's answer would be.

"Yep, first thing in the morning. I figure I better leave before I get my other ear chewed off."

Lynes couldn't help but laugh. Andrea continued, "I told Pierre I'd watch out for you, and I done that. Just one more thing I gotta' tell you 'fore I leave."

"What's that?" Lynes wondered what kind of joke Andrea was going to come up with, but then a serious look crossed Andrea's face. Lynes began to worry that it was not going to be a joke after all.

"You know that young girl that's been trying to get your attention? And you've been ignoring her? Well, her father is a wild man. He's killed two men who made his daughter unhappy. If you want to keep your scalp, you better start paying attention to her." Andrea remained solemn as he studied the look on Lynes's face. Lynes's eyes widened; fear and worry etched his face. Having achieved the result he was looking for, Andrea burst into laughter.

"I got you again, Chiot. You should have seen the look on your face. Don't worry about Renee's father. Smoky is one good man. He told me Renee is interested in you, and that she even made you a plaid shirt. They are a very good family. I assured Smoky that I would put in a good word for Renee. She really likes you."

Lynes was a little perturbed that Andrea had fooled him, but it was something he expected from Andrea anyway. With a sheepish expression on his face, Lynes waved goodby to his friend and left to tend to Cheval.

The "Little Iron Horse" was quick to trot to the edge of the corral when Lynes approached. Cheval had become accustomed to a couple of carrots and a sugar cube, followed by a brushing and other grooming. Lynes had gained the stallion's trust in the many hours that he had spent patiently trying to saddle the spirited horse. That day Lynes thought, it's time to saddle him up and see how he rides.

The horse stood calmly tied to the training post as Lynes walked out of the animal shelter with the saddle in hand. The "Little Iron Horse" gave no sign that he was the least bit disturbed by Lynes's approach. Speaking softly, Lynes raised the saddle to Cheval's back, but the horse moved skittishly away. At Lynes's third attempt to place the saddle on the stallion, he heard a voice from the edge of the corral, "He'll let you ride him without a saddle."

Lynes turned to see Renee sitting on the top rail of the corral fence, her legs dangling over, swinging back and forth under her long black dress. Slightly agitated by the interruption, Lynes wondered how she came to that conclusion. "What makes you think that?"

"I just know." Renee hopped off the top rail like a bronco buster. "Here, want me to show you?" She reached down and grabbed the back of her dress, pulling it up between her legs, revealing her leggings and shapely thighs. "Now, hold on there."

Lynes raised his voice to a little less than a holler. "Have you been messing around with my horse?" He already knew the answer. His anger was kindled as Renee looked affectionately at him.

"I was just trying to help. I could see how much you like this horse."

Lynes thought about the plaid shirt she had made for him and slowly smiled. He remembered Andrea's warning about Smoky. Renee's wide dark eyes sparkled at Lynes's smile. His words came softer now. "Is there anything else I should know about my horse?"

"He works well with a hackamore, and he's in love with my mare."

Lynes laughed. Trusting that Renee was telling him the truth, he slowly got on the back of his horse. He smiled proudly down at the teasing girl. The smile abruptly left his face when the stallion leaped forward at a run, almost unseating his rider. Lynes grabbed a handfull of mane to regain his seat. Jerking back on the rawhide reins, Lynes brought Cheval's head up. The horse then reared, causing Lynes to slide backwards, landing on his backside in the dirt. While Lynes caught his breath, Renee doubled up in laughter.

Brushing himself off, Lynes thought, what happened? What the hell is she laughing about? Angry and embarrassed, Lynes brushed off the dust and questioned Renee, "What the hell happened? I thought you said he could be ridden. Go ahead, show me."

Lynes was well schooled on how to care for and handle a well trained horse, but he knew very little about hackamore training. He was about to get a lesson. Renee's father Smoky was well known in Saskatchewan as the finest horse trainer in the Province, and he passed much of his knowledge on to his daughter. Renee spent the rest of the afternoon showing Lynes how to ride and control his "Little Iron Horse." As the sun began to set on the Metis settlement, the couple's physical attraction to each other as well as their friendship began to grow.

In the following months, Lynes quit his job at the stables so he could contribute more to the Metis community and spend more time with Renee. As the days grew shorter, Lynes began looking forward to the job he had signed up for earlier that spring.

To Lynes, the sawmill had become a giant gluttonous Mistik Windigo (Tree Cannibal). With each log he pulled onto the bull chain, he envisioned the forests he loved being devoured. He looked up at the burner throwing smoke and sparks into the air. The fumes burned his nostrils. As Lynes gazed down into the muddy waters of the North Saskatchewan River, he recalled his grandfather's forewarning, "When all the trees are cut down, when all the animals have been hunted, when all the waters are polluted, when all the air is unsafe to breathe, only then will you discover that you cannot eat money."

Lynes felt as if he was ignoring his grandfather's warning as he fed Mistik Windigo. When those thoughts came to him, he would pray to Kice Manito (God) for humanity's redemption. His hours on the catwalk resembled in some ways the Vision Quest practiced by his mother's people. Many questions were answered in those hours of prayer, including what path he must take to seek justice for his people.

Sheets of ice glittered in the sun along the banks of the North Saskatchewan River. Silver vapors, forming a ghostly mist hovering above the water, rose from the logs surrounding Lynes. The noon whistle was about to blow, and already the sun was sinking in the west. Thick frost blanketed the trees and earth. Lynes knew it wasn't going to be long before he would be hauling supplies to the lumber camps up North.

In the past few months, Lynes had come to feel like the Metis settlement was his home. However, Lynes, in keeping with his nature, longed for more than the comfort and security of the settlement. Subconsciously, he missed the fight for survival that challenged him in the wilderness. As soon as ice covered the North Saskatchewan River, Lynes would once again face the perils and dangers of the Northwoods.

During the few short months that Lynes lived in the Metis community, Rudy's father and Smoky kept him well informed about the actions of the government to displace the Metis people. Lynes's grandfather's stories about the Northwest Rebellion had related very little about the Metis predicament. The new information he learned and his own experiences influenced Lynes's perception of the Canadian government. He began to view that government as the enemy of the Metis people as well as the enemy of his mother's people. Lynes thought, I think like a First Nation's people and a Metis. I must learn how the white man thinks?

Lynes's negative experiences in Prince Albert made him wary of a culture he did not yet understand. He decided that he would further his understanding in the spring as soon as he had finished hauling supplies to the logging camps.

The subzero temperatures that are common in northern Saskatchewan turned the North Saskatchewan River into a solid ice highway, linking it up with hundreds of miles of tributaries. Relieved of his job as a mill worker, Lynes was placed on the company ledger as a teamster, hunter, and interpreter. He was about to embark upon the job he had been anticipating all summer.

Renee stood silent as Lynes harnessed up the team of horses that would carry him into the northern forest. She had heard tales of the hardships and perils that faced the freighters traveling alone in the wilderness. Although she was confident in Lynes's abilities, her concern for his safety preyed on her mind. She was glad she had accompanied Lynes to Prince Albert to see him off on his journey.

Large snowflakes began to settle on the fur-bordered hoods that framed the faces of the young couple as they prolonged their parting. Their embrace was encumbered by the heavy clothing that protected them from the bitter cold. Still, the intensity of their embrace expressed their deep love for each other. As Lynes climbed aboard the cutter and urged the team forward, Renee, as was her habit of getting in the last word, hollered out, "Be careful, sweetheart."

Without looking back, Lynes smiled and waved his hand in recognition of her advice. Within minutes, the only sound Lynes heard was the rattle of the harnesses and the swish of the runners slicing through the crusty snow. White flakes began to build upon the backs of the horses as they effortlessly pulled the cutter upriver. Without a sound, the caulked shoes on the horses' hooves broke through the snow to grip the ice. Lynes felt a kind of peacefulness as he left humankind behind. If only for a short while, he would leave behind the emotional turbulence of the past eight months and return to the quiet solitude of the wilderness. His spirits were rekindled as he consciously attuned his senses to every movement, sound, and sign surrounding him. He passed many abandoned log landings as he wound his way upriver. Twelve hours out of Prince Albert, Lynes noted that every marketable tree within profitable distance from the landing on the river had made its way to the mill. It would be twelve more hours at his present pace before he would reach a landing stacked with logs. Once there, he would leave the river and follow an ice road frequently used to haul logs to the landing. The first leg of his journey would end when he reached a group of temporary buildings that housed thirty-six robust lumberjacks, two cooks, and a young woman who helped in the kitchen and dining hall.

The snowflakes began to fall in a veil of white, limiting Lynes's vision to just inches beyond the horses' breaths. Lynes climbed off the cutter and slowly began to lead the team along the riverbank. He patiently forged forward, determined to reach his goal. The biggest danger for freighters was the thin ice where tributaries entered the river. Lynes remained alert for any danger or obstacle in his path.

Pausing, Lynes gently pulled back on the reins, bringing the team to a gradual halt. A large shadow appeared on the riverbank. Like the flash of the northern lights, the shadow turned on and off, disappearing and reappearing again through the blinding veil of snow. There was only one critter in the Northwoods that size; it had to be Yapi-Moswak (a moose). Having been ingrained with his mother's and grandfather's respect for the spirit of the moose, Lynes walked slowly back to the cutter and retrieved his 1896 Winchester from under the seat. He had purchased the rifle after getting Sgt. Major Marshall's permission. After all, his job as a hunter required him to supply fresh meat to the camps. It was a Metis and Cree legend that the moose gives himself for food to the hunter who will treat him with respect and reverence. Lynes thanked the spirit of the moose for supplying him with fresh meat. No more than three hours passed and Lynes had the fresh meat loaded on the cutter and covered with a prime moose hide.

106

The thick snow flurry had lightened up, and Lynes was able to continue at his normal pace, stopping only long enough to rest the horses from time to time. Days are short in northern Saskatchewan when winter grips the land, and the snowstorm night was black as pitch. Casting eerie shadows as it danced to the rhythm of the horses' gait, the lantern hung from a pole that extended out from the cutter's tongue. Ever alert, Lynes caught a flash of movement just beyond the shadow's edge. Instantly, Lynes recalled the story Pierre had told of the pirates on the Shellbrook River. Crouching down so he would make a smaller target, Lynes readied his Winchester. Again, from the other side of the cutter, he glimpsed another movement beyond the lantern's light. The excitement of the horses verified Lynes's concern. The animals' natural instinct to run from danger was checked by Lynes as he only gave them rein enough to trot at an easy gait. Lynes experienced a kind of exhilaration that triggered his response to danger. Like his father, it was not in his charcter to run from trouble. After a short while, Lynes pulled the team to a halt and jumped off the cutter, intending to creep to the riverbank to lie in wait for an adversary. Then he looked down at the fresh fallen snow and began to laugh as he walked around the cutter. It was surrounded by wolf tracks.

"I've been around the white man too long. I let a pack of hungry wolves excite me and my horses." Lynes took a long logging chain and attached it to the back of the cutter. He then tied the front leg of the moose to the end of the chain. By his actions, Lynes diverted the wolves' attention to the back of the cutter and away from the horses' awareness. The trio continued on through the night.

The sun struggled to cast its light through the silver gray skies as dawn began to break on the North Saskatchewan River. A light snow fell as the temperature began to drop. As Lynes looked over the wide frost-covered backs of his faithful team, he could see far in the distance. Forests lined the banks of the Kisiskaciwani. He stopped to listen. Rumbling sounds and voices could be heard in the icy air. Lynes knew that no more than a mile ahead he would spot the landing he was looking for. And sure enough, just around a bend in the river, the landing loomed into view. Logs were stacked twenty feet high where Lynes left the river. A two-horse team, with two twenty- foot log sleds stacked twelve feet high sat on the ice road where one of the sleds was being unloaded.

As Lynes pulled up onto the landing, he was accompanied by the landing boss holding on to the halter of his lead horse. The landing boss led the team a safe distance from the log deck and walked back to greet Lynes. The boss was a big man with a flaming red beard tucked into his parka hood. His red beard, mustache, and eyebrows were covered with frost from his breath. A generous smile that could have been seen from the other side of the river shone through the frosty face. The man's Scottish brogue and booming voice could be heard above the rumbling of the logs as they rolled off the logging sled.

"Damn glad to see you, laddie. Follow that log sled when he's done unloading. Camp's a couple miles up trail."

Lynes nodded his head, indicating he understood the instructions. The big Scotsman started to walk away, but he turned and walked back to Lynes and slapped him on the leg. "Damn if it ain't good to see you, laddie." Lynes felt like a mule had kicked him in the leg as he gingerly rubbed the targeted limb.

As Lynes was waiting for the log sled to leave the landing, he was surrounded by a beehive of activity mingled with the acrid smell of fresh cut timber. The extensive quantity of bleeding and barked logs emitted a sweet-sour odor that clung to the air that encircled the landing. When Lynes left the landing, he also left the sweet-sour odor behind. In its place, Lynes began to sniff the pungent smoke from the camp. The runners of the cutter fit perfectly in the trenches cut into the ice road. Once again, Lynes was impressed by how effortlessly his team pulled the loaded sled. In less than thirty minutes, he arrived at the camp. In the still cold air, a cloak of smoke hovered over the logging camp. Three log buildings about thirty-five feet long and sixteen feet wide were huddled together in an immense landscape of stumps and forest debris. A fourth building about half the size of the others stood off by itself. Between the buildings, two huge stacks of firewood that furnished the fuel for the kitchen and bunkhouses, dominated the landscape. Fifty feet from those buildings were two horse shelters and a shelter housing logging equipment and a blacksmith shed. The center building was the kitchen, eatery, medical center, and sleeping quarters for the cooks and the young woman who helped in the kitchen and served meals to the lumberjacks. The fourth building housed the company store and office plus the camp foreman. Products in the store consisted of clothing, boots, caulks, soap and toiletries, dried fruits, pemmican, candy, tobacco, among other items. The company store charged twice as much in the bush for products as it did in town.

Two tables, each long enough to seat twelve men on either side elbow-to-elbow, were placed on either side of the dining hall. A big Monarch cook stove, a grill, a pantry, and a huge table occupied the end of the building. Lynes entered the dining hall to inform the cook that his supplies had arrived. The cook was a man of medium build wearing a wool stocking cap pulled down to his ears. His eyes were like a rodent, and his nose like that of W. C. Fields. The busy cook peered over his shoulder at Lynes as he carefully slid a pan full of biscuits into the oven. Lynes didn't understand what the man said, but those at the other end of the dining hall heard him loud and clear.

"Whadayawant?"

The warmth of the dining room coupled with the pleasant aroma of the cooking food tempted Lynes to say, whatever you're cooking, but he got the impression from the tone of Cookie's voice that he didn't have time for small talk. "I'm here with supplies from Prince Albert."

"It's about time." Cookie was getting low on syrup and sugar and knew the lumberjacks would get grumpy without their sweets. He was so happy to see Lynes that he almost smiled. After wiping his hands on the multi-stained apron that reached from his chest to his knees, Cookie sent the second cook for help to unload the supplies. He then walked quickly up to Lynes. His voice had the ring of authority, "Pull them supplies up to that door and come on back in for some hot coffee."

Lynes was more than happy to oblige. When he walked through the doorway, Cookie motioned for him to sit at the table nearest the kitchen. A coffee pot, a full cup of steaming hot coffee, and a full place setting were waiting for him. By the time the coffee cooled off enough to drink, the young serving woman had his plate filled with flapjacks and sizzling hot slices of salt pork. Also on the table was an array of other foods--a bowl of warm applesauce (made from dried apples), syrup, berry preserves, a bowl of sugar, and a bowl of hot oatmeal. Cookie instructed Lynes to sit there and take his time at the table, and he then hurried outside to help unload his supplies. Boxes and barrels marked for Ness Camp, along with moose meat, found their way to the pantry. Lynes felt like he should be helping, but he relented to the bounty in front of him. The oatmeal bowl was soon emptied, and Lynes was working on his third plate of flapjacks when all the supplies for Ness Camp were finally secured in Cookie's pantry. Only then did Cookie sit down next to Lynes and pour himself a cup of coffee.

"You must be plumb tuckered. When you're done eatin', Ron here (He pointed to the second cook.) will find you an empty bunk if you want to get some shuteye. I'll have him wake you up for dinner. Don't worry about your critters; they're taken care of."

Lynes welcomed Cookie's proposal. Twenty-six hours on the river without sleep, the heat from the cook stove, and a full belly, made his eyelids feel like they were made of lead. He thanked Cookie for his hospitality, and when he finished his sixth flapjack, the second cook took him to the bunkhouse. On the way, Ron expressed his own appreciation for bringing them fresh meat. "Thanks for the moose. Ain't had fresh meat for a while. I think we kilt everything within a hundred miles." He went on to tell Lynes how lucky he was to show up in time to see the Bull of the Woods fight.

Entertainment in the logging camps consisted of competition between the men. Usually, it was a competition of skills needed to be a lumberjack. However, other forms of entertainment also came into the mix, for example, who could tell the tallest tale, and who was the toughest man in the woods.

Because logging was one of the most dangerous occupations on earth, lumberjacks were viewed as being healthy robust men inclined to be adventuresome and fearless, a reputation they were proud to preserve. "The Bull of the Woods" in Ness Camp was Carl Jelstrum, a twenty-five-year-old Norwegian immigrant. He came to Canada when he was sixteen years old and worked in logging camps from Quebec to British Columbia. Carl's deep blue eyes, fair hair, average size, and clean-shaven appearance belied the Norwegian's toughness so that no one would suspect that he earned the title of "The Bull of the Woods." Seven miles upriver in the Campbell Camp, they, too, had a Bull of the Woods. Lynes had made it to Ness Camp in time to watch the two titans of the timber settle the question of who, in fact, was the true Bull of the Woods.

"Get your ass out of that bunk if you want something to eat."

Lynes didn't know who woke him up. By the time he became aware of his surroundings, all he saw were lumberjacks leaving the bunkhouse like it was on fire. Alarmed, Lynes darted outside into the darkness and saw everyone in camp gathered around the dining room door. The men were just joking, laughing, and horsing around while standing outside the dining hall. As raucous as it was outside the hall, that all changed when the door opened and the men filed in. Not a word was spoken. Each man had his place at the tables which was changed only by mutual agreement. Cookie had a seat close to the kitchen reserved for Lynes. The tables were set so that there was no need to ask someone to pass something. The only voices to be heard were those of Cookie and the young woman serving the tables. There wasn't so much as a whisper among the lumberjacks. Within fifteen minutes, Lynes found himself the only diner in the place. Wondering if there was some kind of activity that prompted the men to hurriedly leave the dining hall, Lynes asked Cookie why everyone seemed to be in such a hurry. Cookie looked down at Lynes like a teacher looking down at a disruptive student.

"This ain't no place to lollygag around. Those jacks know my rules. "No jaw jacking. Get full and get out." "'Course you can take your time, young fella, you're not going to be here long enough to get in my way."

Lynes took another bite of bread, thanked Cookie, and left the dining hall. The lanterns on the horse shelters cast long moving shadows like phantoms in the night. The lights reminded Lynes that the care of his horses was in others' hands. Knowing he would not be comfortable going to bed without checking on his team, he walked over to the horse barn. Much to his pleasure, his faithful team were standing in front of a hay-filled manger and both were covered with blankets. His cargo sled with its load secured was tucked under the equipment shed, ready for the twelve-mile trip to Campbell Camp. A couple of horses down from Lynes's team, a teamster was brushing down one of his horses. He peered around the rump of his horse.

"Nice team you got there."

"They belong to the company," Lynes answered.

"Ya, they got some good stock, but they ain't got nothin' that could out pull my kids." He slapped his horse on the rump as he walked around to Lynes. "Fact is, there ain't a team in Saskatchewan that could out pull 'em." He waited for Lynes's response. Lynes just shook his head in agreement.

Not getting an adequate reply gave the boisterous teamster the opportunity he desired to spill the tall tale that had won him first place among teamsters. "In fact, I had a pullin' contest with the Centipede. Pulled it backwards for ten miles before it ran out of steam." The Phoenix Centipede was a massive steam-driven hauler with runners in front and tracks in the back. It could pull thirty sleds stacked high with logs. Lynes had never seen or heard of the Centipede. He tried to look impressed and again shook his head in agreement. The teamster broke into laughter and slapped Lynes on the back.

"You ain't met the boys in the bunkhouse!"

A stranger in a logging camp was like a chicken in the coop. It gets pecked on until it finds its place among the other chickens. It was another form of entertainment the loggers used to distract their attention from the daily dangers of the job and from the miserable working and living conditions. An old logger, reflecting upon the years he had worked in logging camps, stated, "If I had to choose today to spend six months in jail or six months in a logging camp, I'd pick the jail."

Lynes enjoyed listening to the teamster. It reminded him of his friend Andrea Beauchene. When Lynes and the teamster entered the bunkhouse, the man put his arm around Lynes's shoulder like a mother hen protecting her chicks. "Look here, boys! This here's Lynes. Brought in our supplies from Prince Albert."

The response was a mixture of grumbling praise and indifference from the bunkhouse occupants. The men were recovering from the rigors forced upon them by a hard day's labor in harsh elements. Lynes was stricken by the pungent odor that was the result of more than twenty-five virile young men, overloaded with testosterone, all stacked into a building like cordwood. The walls of the crude dormitory were lined three high with bunks big enough to accommodate a lumberjack and all of his worldly possessions. Lanterns cast their light on bright red suspenders hooked to canvas pants hanging on the ends and sides of the bunks. Black and red mackinaws (wool shirts) hanging up to dry added to the color that was characteristic of the lumberjack. (As a safety factor, lumberjacks wore bright colors that enabled them to see each other easily in the bush.) In every unused space overhead, caulked boots hung to dry. Near the wood-burning heater in the center of the bunkhouse, five men sat playing cards, three still in their logging gear, and two in their wool long johns. Another group of men near the end of the bunkhouse was singing a song in a language Lynes didn't understand. A fiddler who had mastered his art accompanied the singer. As Lynes made his way to the bunk he had been assigned, he studied each lumberjack he passed, wondering which one of them was the Bull of the Woods. Recognizing the red-bearded man lounging on a middle bunk, Lynes stayed well out of arm's reach, remembering the vigorous slap on his leg.

Morning arrives early in a Northwest logging camp. Lynes was awakened by loud voices and the rustling sound of hurrying men readying themselves to challenge the day. At 4:00 AM, the crisp morning air was invigorating as Lynes stood waiting for the dining hall doors to open. Cookie's words echoed in his mind, "Get full and get out."

By 4:45 AM, the bunkhouses were empty, and the loggers were loaded on log sleds and on the way to their cuttings. Lynes strode to the horse shed to harness up his team and ready himself for the eight-mile trip to Campbell Camp. It would be an easy drive, mostly on the ice road and only a short while on the river. The clear sharp ring of the blacksmith's hammer and the bellows' roar broke the morning silence. It occurred to Lynes that it might be a good idea to have the shoes on his team checked out since a smithy was so close at hand. He drove his team the short distance to the smithy's shed. The man's back was turned when Lynes entered the shed.

"Would you have time to check out my team this morning?"

When the smithy turned around, Lynes was taken aback by the youthfulness of the figure before him. Bobby Hogan was only a couple of years older than he was. Hogan was not a big man, but he had acquired the strength of a blacksmith from seven years of servitude

113

under a brutish master from Birmingham, England. From the age of eleven, he had learned the science of metallurgy and was a master at his trade. His dark brown eyes didn't have the sparkle and innocence of youth; there was a hardness in them, and his gaze made Lynes uncomfortable. Lynes was more than a little surprised by the smithy's answer.

"If you can talk Cookie out of a pot of coffee, I'll take a look at them."

Lynes wasn't sure what Cookie's response would be to a pot of coffee, but he accepted Bobby's deal. Cookie readily handed a hot steaming pot of coffee to Lynes and commented, "That god damn kid's got a hollow leg when it comes to coffee."

Bobby had a horse's hoof on his knee when Lynes returned with the coffee. He continued inspecting the horse's hoof with his hoof pick. "Just put it over there by the forge."

Lynes smiled as he set the coffeepot down beside one that had been recently emptied. He thought, Yep, he must have a hollow leg.

Bobby laid the hoof pick down as carefully and as positively as if it were a Stradivarius. The pick had its place among the other hand tools that were placed precisely in line as if they were on display. Observing Bobby's idiosyncrasy, Lynes scrutinized his surroundings. There wasn't so much as a horseshoe nail that wasn't in perfect order. Booby grabbed a bucket from a stack of buckets that had all their handles hanging identically to one another. He took care to set the bucket by the forge, turning it several times until it sat exactly as he thought it should be.

"Here, sit down." (He motioned to the bucket.) "Have a cup of coffee."

Lynes sat down as Bobby carefully filled a cup he had precisely placed in front of the bucket. The hardness gradually left Bobby's eyes as he stared a full thirty seconds at Lynes before he spoke. "My guess is, this isn't your first time in the bush."

Lynes answered, "I was raised about ten smokes north of here."
"Smokes?"
"Wow! I thought only aborigines lived up here."
"I live near my mother's village."
"Boy! You sure don't look like an Indian."

114

Lynes became defensive. "Boy! You sure don't look like a blacksmith!"

Realizing he had unintentionally offended his young guest, Bobby laughed and changed the subject. His intentions were to engage Lynes in conversation until the coffeepot was empty. Bobby enjoyed his coffee much better if he was having a pleasant conversation. "Are you going to be here tomorrow (Sunday) to watch the Pollack kick Carl's ass? I got my money on the Pollack."

The Polle's name was Alex Polieski, but he preferred to be called "Bull" in reference to his claim that HE was the Bull of the Woods. Weighing nearly 300 pounds, the Pole had never been defeated in a Bull of the Wood's wrestling match in his ten years as a lumberjack. He bragged that the only logger greater than he was the legendary Joe Mafraw. (Often spelled in various ways). Joe Mafraw is Canada's equivalent to America's Paul Bunyan. During one of the many competitions between the Ness Camp and the Campbell Camp, Bull had laid down a Bull of the Wood's challenge to the Ness Camp for an opponent. Carl Jelstrup was the only man to accept that challenge.

Lynes's intentions were to be back to Ness Camp before dark that evening if everything went well during the day. "Yes, I'll be back here to spend the night if I can get on the road right away." Lynes was hoping Bobby would take the hint.

"I guess you'll be bringing back a couple of passengers from what I hear."

"Yeh, that's OK. I just want to get on the road." Lynes was done throwing out hints.

Bobby stood up and took a long indulgent sip from his cup. "I gotcha. If you get back tonight, drop by for a cup of coffee." The blacksmith picked up his hoof pick and walked out to the horses. Lynes remained seated, enjoying the warmth from the forge and his coffee. He had a big smile on his face as he watched Bobby leave the shed.

Campbell Camp looked very much like Ness Camp. Lynes glanced up at the sun before he entered the dining hall. He mentally calculated where the sun had to be when he left Campbell Camp so that he would be back in Ness Camp in time for dinner. Lynes was pleased that the cook was in a hurry to get the supplies in his pantry and in the company store. When the last box was taken from the supply shed, Lynes recalled the conversation he had with Bobby. He turned to the camp cook.

"I understand I'm going to have a couple of passengers to transport to Ness Camp."

"No. They'll be going back to Prince Albert. Pull the sled behind the store."

Two crudely built boxes lay under an accumulation of frost and snow. As the boxes were being loaded on the supply sled, it struck Lynes that these were his passengers. Lynes didn't feel the need to know how his passengers had acquired their condition. His concern was that their souls (Manitowak) were also going along for the trip. There was no confusion concerning the dead as far as Lynes was concerned. His grandfather and his mother, as well as the Christian missionaries, had instilled in him reverence and respect for the souls of humankind. When Lynes left Campbell Camp, he was speaking to the souls of his cold, silent passengers. As he spoke, he heard in the distance, the sound of Saskanotin (the Chinook wind) whispering across the devastation left by the woodsman's axe. Lynes brought his excited team to a halt and turned to the sound of the Chinook. The warm west wind overcame the sub-arctic cold, and like the comfort of the blacksmith's forge, it radiated its warmth upon the young trapper's face. Lynes felt a burden had been lifted from him when the west wind passed. It came to Lynes in a vision that now that these men were being taken home to their loved ones, the Wind Spirit set their souls free to be with their ancestors in the northern lights.

Two hours before the sunset and two hours before sunrise are the coldest times of the day. Traveling along, Lynes began to feel the cold creep in as he approached Ness Camp. The distant sound of the blacksmith's hammer reminded Lynes of Bobby's invitation. When he backed his sled into the equipment barn and unhooked the team, a voice rang out from the blacksmith shed.

"Coffee's on."

There was no retort from Lynes as he drove his team to the horse shed and placed blankets over the critters' backs. An armful of hay and a bucket of grain were their reward for a job well done. Lynes was looking forward to the heat from the forge as he hurried into the blacksmith's shed. The bucket was exactly where it had been when Lynes last sat there, and an empty cup sat exactly where it had been when it was last set before him. Lynes did not find it humorous when Bobby joked as he filled Lynes's cup. The blacksmith was laughing as he spoke, "Your passengers weren't very good company on your way down here, were they?"

Bobby's eyebrows raised in bewilderment when he looked to Lynes for a response. Lynes's eyes seemed to focus on the flames dancing in the forge. It appeared to Bobby that Lynes was in a trance; his face was expressionless, and his voice sent a shiver down Bobby's spine.

"Their souls are free. Cipayak-nimitowak (Dancing with their ancestors).

As a recent arrival in Canada, Bobby had not known any First Nations People or Metis. Bobby, like most people from the British Isles, believed the Indian and the Metis were stupid, immoral savages. Such people had little or no understanding or respect for the native cultures and religions. However, Lynes's sincere and reverent response drew empathy and curiosity from the blacksmith. Curious as to Lynes's response, Bobby asked him to explain what he meant. He was genuinely impressed by Lynes's spirituality; therefore, Lynes was pleased that the blacksmith was showing an interest in his culture and religion. The two men talked until the coffeepot was empty, and the dining hall doors were opened.

There was excitement in the Ness Camp the following morning. The normal stoic-like attitudes and demeanors of the lumberjacks gave way to boisterous gaiety. Lynes raised himself in his bunk and strained his neck to see who it was that was attracting so much attention. Through the crowd of men gathered around a bunk, Lynes caught his first sight of the Ness Camp challenger to Alex "Bull" Polieski. The whispers and light chatter at breakfast was quieted by Cookie banging on the bottom of a large tin pan. One of the loggers hollered out, "I hope you got another set of teeth; you're gonna need 'em!" The Norwegian laughed and took a gulp of steaming hot tea.

When Lynes and Bobby left the dining hall, Bobby had a full pot of coffee in his hand, and Lynes had several rolled up flapjacks in his pouch. Both men preferred the quiet company of the blacksmith shed to the noise and odor of the bunkhouse. Besides, they would be the first to see the Campbell Camp log sleds coming down the ice road.

The buildings cast their shadows on the blanket of white that covered Ness Camp. The long dark night surrendered once again to the welcomed morning's light. A distant sound caught Lynes's ear. It would fade away and then return like gusts of wind through the trees. As the sound grew closer, it was clear that it was the voices of men in song. They were singing a parody to the popular song, "I've Been Working on the Railroad," that went like the following:

"I've been working for the log boss trying to make a dime.

The way I'm treated by the log boss is a bloody crime.

I can hear him screaming at me, "You gotta get more trees down.

The only way to please him is send him back to town.

Send him back to town. Send him back to town. Send the log boss back to town.

Send him back to town. Send him back to town. Hell, lets all go back to town.

There's nothin' tougher than a logger; I'm tellin' you that it's true.

He survives on camp food; ain't nothin' he can't chew.

He can fight a buzz saw and give it twenty turns to start.

There just ain't nothin' stronger than a logger's heart.

Yah, a logger's tough. Yah, a logger's tough. A loggin man don't know fear.

Yah, a logger's tough. Yah, a logger's tough. He can drink a case of whiskey and a boxcar load of beer."

The singing stopped, and the men started whooping and hollering when the log sled entered Ness Camp. Before the sled stopped, men started jumping off, some falling on their faces and others staggering in various directions. Although Camp rules were that alcohol was forbidden, it appeared that somehow a good quantity had slipped through on Lynes's supply sled. A circle began to form in front of the chow hall with lumberjacks from the bunkhouses mingling with those from Campbell Camp. Lynes didn't know which of the burly men was Bull until he entered the ring of men.

Bobby whispered in Lynes's ear, "Look at the size of the man, Lynes. Look at the size of the man!"

Bull stood six feet-five inches tall and three and a half feet wide from his shoulders to his thighs. From under a heavy red woolen stocking cap that dangled down to his shoulders, flowed a thick bush of dark brown hair, billowing out like straw in a hurricane. Black bushy eyebrows sat above an almost boyish round face that was masked beneath a scruffy black beard with streaks of gray hiding what little space there was between the head and the shoulders. And in the midst, set wide apart, were dark brown eyes that were reputed to be able to pierce a man's very soul. And so it was that when Lynes's and Bull's eyes met, the young man's mind was flooded with every emotion he had ever known. And even some that were yet to be. Bull maintained his stare into Lynes's eyes until Lynes tore his eyes away. At the same time, Bull removed his heavy machinaw jacket, revealing a black wool shirt underneath. Bull and the log boss from Ness Camp stood in the middle of the circle of men for almost a minute. The loggers began to jeer and shout until Carl finally made himself present. Wearing only a pair of wool pants, Carl stood looking up into the face of his opponent. Seemingly oblivious to the sub-arctic cold, he listened to the log boss give his instructions for the match.

"There ain't going to be no eye-gouging, no biting, no kicking, and no punching. This match is over when somebody quits or can't fight anymore. OK, fellas, let 'er rip."

The log boss's words were no sooner out of his mouth when Bull lunged at Carl. As if he had anticipated Bull's move, Carl spun to one side and moved out of arm's reach. After several lunges by Bull to no avail, Bull stood still and taunted Carl. Carl laughed and made runs at Bull, staying well out of arm's reach. As the jeers and anger in the crowd grew so did the anger build in Bull. Soon, anger became rage as Bull lunged at Carl. At the last instant, Carl crouched down and grabbed Bull around the thighs. When Carl stood up straight, he lifted Bull off the ground. Bull fell forward as his huge arms squeezed Carl's neck, burying Carl's face against his massive chest. Bull then tried to wrap his legs around Carl's torso in the scissors hold, but Carl averted the hold by twisting his body from side to side as he slipped his hand inside Bull's grasp. Fifteen minutes passed as the two grappled in the snow, and then Carl had his forearm between Bull's arm and his chest. The more Bull struggled to wrap his legs around Carl, the more of Carl's arm interfered with Bull's grip. Finally, after a half hour of Bull's pinning Carl down in the snow, Carl got his right arm and shoulder free above Bull's arms. Bull was still not able to wrap his legs around Carl. Unable to control Bull's hulk, Carl bore the pain of Bull's weight and bear hug, squirming upward inch by inch at each attempt the wrestler made to get a better grip. Another half hour passed. By now Bull's grip was around Carl's chest. He had squeezed the breath from many a man with his bear hug, but Carl wasn't just any man. With his arms now free, Carl gripped his own left wrist, left palm facing outward against Bull's chin, pushing Bull's head back, exposing what little neck Bull had hidden under his beard. Bull refused to stop the bear hug, jerking violently to expel the last bit of air from Carl's lungs. At each jerk, Bull's head was pressed further back by fractions of an inch. Now Carl had his legs wrapped around Bull. It was almost two hours into the match when Bull's neck was stretched as far back as it could go. Clouds of breath began to flow with force and more rapidly from Bull's lungs. Carl's breath was evenly spaced vapors melting into the sub-arctic atmosphere. His breathing was as if he were lounging on his bunk. The circle of spectators began to thin out and only an occasional call of encouragement was heard from the bored loggers. Bull's grunts and growls could be heard among the laughter and raucous conversations of the lumberjacks.

Bobby turned to Lynes, "Hell, this could go on all day. I'm gonna go for a cup of coffee and a warm up."

"I'll join you." Lynes said. He had already concluded that the big man on top was going to win. Lynes and Bobby headed for the blacksmith shed. Bobby was carefully pouring out his second cup when a roar came from the men. Cups in hand, Lynes and Bobby hurried to see what caused the crowd to come alive. To their astonishment, they saw Carl latched onto Bull's neck. His right shoulder pressed against the right side of Bull's neck and his left arm applying pressure on the left side of Bull's neck. And then both arms locked under Bull's chin. A beast like gnarl came from Bull as he tried to break Carl's grip. Shaking his head violently from side to side, eyelids blinking, his attempts to free himself becoming more feeble, Bull dropped his massive arms to his sides. Carl released his deadly hold. As Bull lay unconscious in the snow, his breath created gentle clouds as if he was in a restful sleep. When Bull awakened, unaware that he had been unconscious, he insisted that the contest continue. Bull would never admit that he had been defeated and would continue lauding himself as the "Bull of the Woods."

The rest of the morning and throughout the day, Lynes and Bobby shared their thoughts as young people do, each learning from the other the values by which they had become the individuals they were. As an indentured servant, Bobby had watched his master grow incredible wealth through hard work, ingenuity, personal relationships, and the labor of others. This model would be the principles by which he would achieve his own goals. As Lynes listened to the aspirations of Bobby, he began to understand the culture into which he had been thrust. Unlike Bobby, Lynes's aspiration was not the gaining of wealth. His spiritual upbringing by his mother and grandfather instilled in him the concept that all humankind share in all that God (Kisi Manito) gives them. Rather, Lynes's ambition was to seek justice for all people and to make life better for his own people. When Lynes left Ness Camp the next morning, he was already formulating a plan on how he was going to achieve his goals.

About the Author

He was a husband, father, little brother, big brother, Uncle, grandfather and great grandfather. Most of all he was a friend to many. He loved them like his family with all of his being. Guy was one of the toughest of men and the most generous of heart.

He worked hard and played harder. He enjoyed fishing, hunting, racing motorcycles, & so much more.

On a few occasions he would gather ingredients and materials to throw together a batch or two of shine. Shared also by a handful of homered persons.

Finally, he seemed to get a kick out of educating himself and discussing both religion and politics. Stopping by to say hello was almost guaranteed to engage in one or the other.

Sharing his experiences with his children and grandchildren was by far important beyond words. Some may say this was Guys way of modeling what it takes to "kick ass and take names."

On a crisp December morning
It was the opening day,
for the winter run of steelhead.
And I was on my way.

With my fishing pole and gear in hand
I took a little sip.
Then hiked on to Fall City
On my little fishing trip.

But soon my footsteps floundered
I was chilled down to my core
A ghostly mist engulfed the town
Like I'd never seen before.

Through the haze I heard the drums
And the flutes shrill filled the air.
I heard chants to the Moon Child
Twas the Indians sacred prayer.

Printed in the United States
By Bookmasters